F. C. Armstrong

The Naval Lieutenant

A Nautical Romance in Three Volumes: Vol. II.

F. C. Armstrong

The Naval Lieutenant
A Nautical Romance in Three Volumes: Vol. II.

ISBN/EAN: 9783337020996

Printed in Europe, USA, Canada, Australia, Japan

Cover: Foto ©Andreas Hilbeck / pixelio.de

More available books at **www.hansebooks.com**

NOW READY.

In Three Vols.

THE NAVAL LIEUTENANT.

By F. C. ARMSTRONG,

Author of " The Two Midshipmen," " The Medora," " The Lily of Devon," " The Queen of the Seas," &c.

In Three Vols.

IT MAY BE TRUE.

By MRS. WOOD.

IN THE PRESS.

In Three Vols. (In October.)

THE MAITLANDS.

In Three Vols. (In October.)

AN OLD MAN'S SECRET.

By FRANK TROLLOPE.

THE FURNISHING OF BED-ROOMS.

HEAL and SON have observed for some time that it would be advantageous to their Customers to see a much larger selection of BED-ROOM FURNITURE than is usually displayed, and that to judge properly of the style and effect of the different descriptions of Furniture, it is necessary that each description should be placed in a separate room. They have therefore erected large and additional Show-Rooms, by which they are enabled not only to extend their show of Iron, Brass, and Wood Bedsteads, and Bed-room Furniture, beyond what they believe has ever been attempted, but also to provide several small rooms for the purpose of keeping complete suites of Bed-room Furniture in the different styles.

Japanned Deal Goods may be seen in complete suites of five or six different colours, some of them light and ornamental, and others of a plainer description. Suites of Stained Deal Gothic Furniture, Polished Deal, Oak, and Walnut, are also set apart in separate rooms, so that customers are able to see the effect as it would appear in their own rooms.

The Stock of Mahogany Goods for the better Bed-rooms, and Japanned Goods for plain and Servants' use, is very greatly increased, the whole forming as complete an assortment of Bed-room Furniture as they think can possibly be desired.

HEAL AND SON'S

ILLUSTRATED CATALOGUE OF

BEDSTEADS, BEDDING,

AND

BED-ROOM FURNITURE,

Sent free by Post.

196, 197, 198, TOTTENHAM COURT ROAD.

THE NAVAL LIEUTENANT.

A NAUTICAL ROMANCE.

IN THREE VOLUMES.

BY

F. C. ARMSTRONG,

Author of " The Two Midshipmen," " The Lily of Devon,"
" The Medora," " The Queen of the Seas," &c., &c.

VOL. II.

London:
T. CAUTLEY NEWBY, PUBLISHER,
30, WELBECK STREET, CAVENDISH SQUARE,
1865.

THE NAVAL LIEUTENANT.

CHAPTER I.

THERE was in truth plenty to do to set all things in order on board La Belle Poule. But the crew belonged to a well-known privateer, were young and active men, and under the guidance of their own mate, Mr. Hawkins, worked with hearty good will. They were besides exceedingly anxious to shew their young skipper their gratitude for their release from the hands of a set of ruthless ruffians, who, when infuriated by drink, would doubtless have killed most of them, or at least condemned them to severe sufferings.

The weather continued thick, the breeze

being fresh, but shifting. Mr. Hawkins thought
the fog would lift with the rising sun. Tom
Darking and a couple of his comrades, were
busy setting the cabin in its usual order; others
were searching every part of the schooner
for arms and ammunition, so that in case of
necessity they might be prepared for a determined resistance. The terrible marks of the
recent fight were washed away, and all other
matters disposed of, so that by the time
daylight dawned everything was tolerably
arranged. The wounded were cared for as
well as circumstances would admit, the entire
crew had provisions and wine served out to
them, and when the fog which arose from
the waters, dispersed, under the influence of a
fine westerly breeze that had sprung up, all
on board were in high spirits.

"Isn't it something wonderful, your honour,"
said Tom Darking, coming up from the cabin
which he and his comrades had rendered
quite tidy, "that we should take the same
privateer that attempted to capture the Cum-

berland. Blow me, but you settled the rascally
skipper's log this time, anyhow."

" Well, it is strange, Tom, and very providential our doing so."

Mr. Hawkins then joined our hero, who
already felt a great liking for the mate of the
Fox. He was a strong, muscular-built man,
with good expressive features, and extremely
well-mannered, in fact, quite above his station
as mate.

" I find this is not your first introduction
to the Belle Poule, Mr. Chamberlain," said
the mate.

" No, indeed; she attempted to capture the
Cumberland Packet, in which I was sailing;
we beat her off, but she had more than fifty
men on board her at that time. What has
become of them ? and besides, she must since
then have captured the Fox."

" I can explain that to you, sir," said the
mate. " After her misadventure with the Cumberland she took two good prizes, and parted
with nearly twenty of her men, to send them

into port. But see, the fog disappears, another time we will talk this over ; we had better get under weigh at once."

" You are right, no time ought to be lost," said our hero.

" I may tell you, however," observed the mate, " that your prize is a valuable one ; she has eight thousand pounds in specie aboard, besides two thousand pounds belonging to poor Capt. Penson, of the Fox."

After the topsails were loosed, and the peak of the mainsail hoisted, the anchor broke ground, and the Belle Poule was under weigh. There was a fine channel, after weathering the island and its reefs of rock, to work through, between the two Penmarks, east and west—from thence to Ushant the run was about ninety miles. The ease with which the Belle Poule worked, and her great speed, delighted the young skipper. She was certainly a very beautiful vessel, very long, and with great beam, and able to engage with any gun-brig afloat.

"Ah," he thought, "If I could only get the command of this craft when I get to England."

Just then they weathered the east point of the island, and stood out for the West Penmarks.

"There's a lugger some four miles to windward," said Mr. Hawkins, handing his glass to the midshipman, "and, I think, a large cutter lying-to further out."

"By Jove! it is not improbable that it is the lugger in which I boarded the schooner— let me see." After a steady look, he exclaimed, "It's the Fraternity. I am sure of it. The rascals, when they cut her adrift last night, must have made sail, and worked out. I should have thought it more likely that they would have made for their own port."

"It's not unlikely," said Mr. Hawkins, "but that they, in a spirit of vengeance, and hoping to re-capture the schooner, make for Brest, to give the alarm, and get some cruiser out to intercept us."

"It is possible; but the cutter I am now looking at is, I think, a French cruizer, and the very same that chased us from the bay of Audierne. If so, we shall not escape without a brush; for she appeared to me a fast craft, and, no doubt, those fellows in the lugger will betray us."

"In that case, sir, we had better prepare to give them a warm reception. We have a very formidable gun amidships, and the only thing we have to guard against is their boarding us. There must be three times or more our number of men aboard the cutter."

"Well, I should think so. The management of the 'midship gun I will leave to you, Mr. Hawkins, and take the wheel myself, if they attack us. Keep an eye upon the lugger, for she will reach the cutter before we come up with her. "Now, Tom," added our hero, "take a spell of the wheel for a while, till I just step down and let our passengers know that there is a chance of another fight, and, if I can, persuade them that there is no fear of a re-capture."

" I'm blowed," muttered Tom, as our hero descended the companion stairs, " If ever they'll take this here craft whilst our skipper, or one of us, remains alive."

" You are right, old chum," said Bill Barker, coming aft, " he is the lad to set foot on an enemy's deck. I never seed such a chuck of a cutlass in my life as he gived the skipper of this here craft. I helped to put him overboard, and his head was only hanging on by a piece of skin."

Mr. Hawkins and the rest of the men were very busy handing up ammunition, &c., &c. There was an abundance of stores. The eighteen-pounder was loaded heavily with grape and canister, and the eight-pounders with round shot. They were only eighteen able men altogether; nevertheless, they felt as confident of success, in case of a contest with the French cruiser, as if their complement exceeded that of the cutter.

On descending to the cabin, our hero found
Mrs. Penson lying on one of the sofas,
propped up with pillows, and Rose Talbot
pouring out for her some coffee she had
boiled, Tom Darking having lighted the
cabin stove.

" Well, you are much better, my dear
friend," said our hero, sitting down, and taking
the coffee Rose instantly poured out for
him.

" Oh, yes, my dear Mr. Chamberlain, I am
quite well, taking everything into consideration. Providence has been very merciful—
though I have lost a kind, good husband in
Captain Penson, I must not murmur, for I
and my beloved child are saved ; but, my
dear boy—excuse my calling you so—how
you have grown, and into such a handsome
man—bless me, what's that?" for the loud
boom of a gun was just then heard. Augustus sprang to his feet, and Rose trembled as
she also started up.

" Don't be alarmed," said our hero to Rose,

"if you do hear some firing—there is no danger. Now I must go."

"Ah, my God!" said Rose, sinking down beside her terrified mother. "More fighting —more danger to those we love."

On reaching the deck, the lieutenant perceived that they were within less than a mile of the cutter, who had let draw her fore sheet, and was standing towards them.

"The lugger has been alongside the cutter, sir," said Mr. Hawkins, "and no doubt those in her have received arms from the cruiser. They know now how few we are, and therefore will try and run us on board."

"It would be the best plan certainly" said our hero, taking his place at the wheel, "but with so fine a working breeze as this, I think I shall baffle them; watch your opportunity, and I'll give you a fair chance of raking her with our shot; never mind her first broadside; watch my signal, I will raise my cap; and now run up our ensign, and stand to your tacks and sheets, my lads."

The two vessels approached each other within musket shot, when the cutter, yawing, fired her broadside guns, all eight-pounders. She was a very large vessel, full of men, and quite a hundred and seventy tons burden. As the Sans Pareil yawed, our hero suddenly luffed up, and the schooner passed under the cutter's stern; as she did so, our hero raised his cap, and the iron shower from the carronade tore across the enemy's deck, hurling several of her crew into eternity, and cutting away the sheets of her foresail and gib, and causing momentary confusion.

As both vessels shot up into the wind, the cutter for want of her foresail and gib, which the men were hauling in to put fresh sheets to, gathered stern way, but continued to fire her side guns, which, however, only cut up the rigging, and made some holes in the sails of the Belle Poule, wounding one man with a splinter.

The two vessels for more than twenty minutes kept up an incessant fire with their broadside guns, till the cutter, having got everything in order, made a most determined attempt to board its opponent, favoured by a slight shift of wind and a squall; but so narrowly did our hero watch every movement, that the cutter's intention was frustrated, though the schooner's jib-boom was carried away in the attempt. Whilst attending to this manœuvre, the lugger was unnoticed. She also made a resolute attempt to board thinking that the Sans Pareil was sure to succeed, but hauled off in time to avoid collision, passing close under the schooner's stern, and firing a dozen muskets into the Belle Poule. One of the men was hauling in a rope close beside our hero ; he was shot dead by this discharge of muskets. One of the balls also passed along the skipper's sleeve, raising the skin from the elbow to the shoulder. It was the last expiring act of the lugger. The eighteen-pounder was double shotted, for the purpose of crippling the cutter, by bringing down her mainsail, but so enraged was Tom

Darking on seeing his comrades fall, and our
hero stagger for a moment, that he and Mr.
Hawkins swung round the gun, and sent its
contents into the lugger's stern, within less
than pistol shot. The balls struck some inches
below the water line, as the vessel was raised
by a wave, and drove in the stern. It filled
rapidly, and, with a wild cry from the doomed
crew, sunk; the miserable remainder of
the Belle Poule's crew going down with her.

Tom Darking then ran up to the skipper,
saying anxiously, "You are hit, sir, the blood
is running from your sleeve."

"Take this handkerchief, Tom," he answered; "tie it tight just above the elbow;
it's a mere scratch, and fortunately my left
arm, and tell Mr. Hawkins to double shot the
gun, and aim, when I run you close, at the
mast head of the cutter."

Both vessels were now a little apart engaged
in repairing damages and splicing ropes.
The schooner's crew had run out a temporary
jib-boom, and cleared away the wreck.

The cutter re-commenced the contest with double-shott·d guns and musketry, but so few were the crew of the schooner that not one man was hit, though the bulwarks and rigging and yards suffered severely.

Watching a favourable opportunity, and giving the wheel to Mr. Hawkins, our hero laid the gun, ran his eye along the sight, and when within pistol shot fired. A loud cheer from his crew attested the result; the mast head of his opponent was knocked into splinters, and down came the immense sail, covering the entire after-deck of the cutter. Paying right off, the Belle Poule passed under the cutter's stern and hailed, calling on the commander to surrender, or they would rake them. The answer was a volley of musketry from the bows and a couple of brass swivels, with balls and old pieces of iron, wounding James Barker, Mr. Hawkins, and our hero, but all very slightly.

Another shower of iron from the eighteen-pounder shortly after, and the impossibility

of their doing anything but run before the
wind, left those in the cutter so completely at the mercy of the schooner's terrible
gun, that one of the officers held out a flag on
a pole as a token of surrender, and then the
firing ceased.

At that moment the attention of our hero
and his crew was attracted by the distant
boom of a very heavy gun, and, looking to
leeward, they beheld a large ship, evidently a
vessel of war, working up to them under a
press of canvass.

" Get me the glass, Tom, make haste ; that's
a frigate.   If it's a French one, our only
safety lies in our heels.   She's three miles
and more to leeward ; that's something."

After a careful look he joyfully exclaimed,
"by Jove, it's the Indefatigable.   Now get
out the small boat, Tom, the large one is
smashed to splinters, and I will board the
cutter, for I am particularly anxious to do
so."

Turning as he spoke, he saw the anxious

pale face of Rose Talbot, looking out from
the companion, and he waved his hand to
her.

"Ah!" said the girl, her eyes resting
upon our hero. "He's safe, thank God! and
the fight is over," and she hurried down to
tell her mother.

Mr. Hawkins had regarded the advancing
frigate with some apprehension, but hearing
our hero say the stranger was the Indefatigable, felt considerably relieved, and
as soon as the midshipman put off for the
cutter he descended into the cabin to let Mrs.
Penson know she need now feel perfectly re-
assured, as no further mischance could occur,
wind and weather excepted, to retard
their reaching their native land.

Our hero was anxious to board the
cutter, not so much to take possession of
his prize, as to find out, if possible, whether
Monsieur de Hauteville had anything to do
with her position in the bay of Audierne and
her giving them chase. As soon as he was

alongside he seized hold of the rigging, and
then sprung upon deck, closely followed by
Tom Darking.

The crew of the Sans Pareil were gathered together in groups, the appearance of the deck
giving evident tokens of the contest; several
dead bodies lay huddled together, and many
of the wounded were sitting pale and haggard-
looking on the deck, but all glared savagely
at the young skipper, and his athletic looking
attendant.

The captain of the Sans Pareil, with a
bandage round his head, and his left arm in
a sling, came up to our hero, and after a
glance of surprise into his youthful countenance, and another at his faded uniform, said—

" Who is it, monsieur, who now commands
the Privateer schooner, La Belle Poule."

" I do, monsieur," returned our hero, "for
the present. I am an officer belonging to his
Britannic majesty's ship Leander."

" Sacre diable ! " muttered the French
skipper, rubbing his head, as if confused, " I

do not comprehend; we have surrendered, at all events, there was no help for it; for you knocked us so about with that confounded eighteen-pound carronade, that we got disabled, for want of our main-sail; but may I ask you a question or two."

"Most undoubtedly, monsieur," said our hero, "if you will in return favour me with a reply to one or two enquiries of mine."

"Parbleu, willingly; now I wish to ask you," began the French skipper, "what vessel captured La Belle Poule?"

"I thought the crew of the lugger had given you that information," said our hero, surprised, "did you not recognise the lugger as the one you chased out of Audierne bay?"

"Is it possible," exclaimed the Frenchman, "we were too hurried; the men in the lugger merely said they belonged to the Belle Poule, which was boarded in the night by a ship's crew of English, and to give them muskets and ammunition, and they would help us to re-take the schooner."

"Then you were stationed, last night," said the lieutenant, "in the bay of Audierne to intercept the escape of some English prisoners who would, if they succeeded in seizing a lugger, run out of the bay steering a northerly course."

"Exactly so," said the mystified French skipper, "I received directions to cruise in the bay, keeping a careful look out to the north and east, and to seize any lugger leaving the bay, and carry the English prisoners to Brest."

"Well, monsieur," returned our hero, "you chased the very lugger we sunk ; myself and three sailors were in her. In the night we boarded the Belle Poule, and with the assistance of an English crew released from her hold, we took the privateer, whose Captain was slain in the fierce contest that took place."

"Tonnerre de diable!" exclaimed the skipper, "you amaze me ; and now you have taken the Sans Pariel, malheureux que je suis."

The crew of the cutter here drew the attention of their skipper to the rapidly advancing ship.

" A French frigate," exclaimed the skipper, with a shout of joy.

" No, monsieur," returned our hero, " an English frigate."

" You know her to be Anglais?" exclaimed the poor skipper, looking cast down.

" Oui, monsieur ; but I have no wish to make you or any of your men prisoners of war. You may put out your boats, take your personal effects, and the wounded, and pull ashore at the back of the Penmarks."

The crew heard the words, and all rushed down below, and in an incredible short time returned upon deck, laden with their effects. Two boats were launched, and into them descended the captain and his crew and the wounded men, the former shaking our hero by the hand, and calling him " un brave garçon."

By this time the English frigate had

reached within two miles of the schooner and
cutter; a wreath of smoke curled out of her
bow port, and the boom of her heavy gun
pealed over the deep.

" This is capital work, sir," said Tom
Darking, " two fine craft, and only one man
killed and two wounded."

" Fortune has favoured us, Tom. You had,
however, better jump into the boat, and go
back to the schooner; tell Mr. Hawkins to
come on board the cutter, and to bring six
hands with him. I will then take the boat
and pull alongside the frigate."

" Aye, aye, sir, but I trust in whatever ship
you goes, you will get Tom Darking a berth.
I should like to stick to the same colours that
your honour fights under."

" Never fear, my man," said our hero, " I
don't forget the pike thrust between my head
and the cutlass of the privateer captain."

" Ah, your honour, we are not half quits
yet. I don't forget your jumping overboard
off the Island of St. Vincent, and keeping me

up till my senses that were knocked out by hitting against a lower stun-sail yard, came back."

"Faith, Tom," said our hero, "that was a near squeak for both, as a brace of sharks had just made up their minds to breakfast upon us; but shove off, and hasten Mr. Hawkins."

The British frigate came majestically along, and when within pistol shot of the two vessels threw her fore-topsail aback, and lay to.

By this time Mr. Hawkins and six hands were on board the cutter, and our hero jumping into the boat, which four men urged through the water, soon gained the side of the Indefatigable.

This frigate, after her action with the Droits de l'Homme, and having narrowly escaped the fate of her consort, had soon repaired her damages, and was again cruising off Brest; this time forming part of Lord Bridport's fleet.

Augustus Chamberlain mounted the side,

and stood upon the deck, surrounded by men and officers all strangers to him, and who regarded him with considerable curiosity, though his faded and well-worn uniform, at all events, proved that he belonged to the British navy.

One of the lieutenants of the Indefatigable at once addressed him, saying, " Sir Edward Pellew will be glad to see you, sir.   He is on the quarter-deck."

" Very good," replied the young man, " I shall be most happy to see a commander I once served under, though only as a volunteer."

Our hero and the lieutenant of the Indefatigable proceeded to the quarter-deck, where Sir Edward Pellew was expecting him. As he approached, our hero at once recognised the commander of the Indefatigable, though rather more than four years had elapsed since he last trod the same deck with him.

Sir Edward looked earnestly into the features of the young midshipman, as though he evidently could not recall the time or the place where he had seen him; there was a misty recollection in the captain's brain that he had before seen the young man who now saluted him respectfully, and then looked up in his face.

" By Jove! I have seen you somewhere or other, sir," said Sir Edward, good humouredly, " pray freshen my memory a little, before I ask you a few questions."

" I was on the deck of the Nymph, Sir Edward, when she fought the Cleopatra; but I served only as a volunteer."

"Ah, by Jove! I remember you now, though not your name. You are the midshipman who, amid a tremendous fire of musketry, ran up the rigging, and cut away the ropes that held the Cleopatra's jib-boom against our mast-head. You saved our mainmast. Oh, yes; it's come back all fresh in my memory now. I thanked you at the time for your gallant service. I am glad to see you," and Sir Edward held out his hand, shaking our hero's kindly. " And now, my young friend, refresh my memory with your name, and tell me all about those two vessels you came from."

Having told his name, our hero, in as brief terms as possible, stated his escape in the lugger, and the taking of the Belle Poule and Sans Pareil.

" By Jove! you're a gallant fellow, Mr. Chamberlain," exclaimed the delighted commander of the Indefatigable, for no one loved gallant and daring exploits more than the future Lord Exmouth. " But come below. I am going to dine, and I must have the pleasure of your company, for I see you have some other details to give. Mr. Spencer," turning to his first lieutenant, " You will join us. By-the-by, I may now, as it has struck my memory, tell you, I saw your name in the last list of promotions sent us. You are appointed third lieutenant of your old ship, the Leander. This list, however, was made out before the news of the failure at Santa Cruz was known in England;

therefore you ought to have received your appointment — it must have reached the Leander months ago."

" I have been absent, Sir Edward," returned our hero, " many months— ever since the night of our attack upon Santa Cruz," and then he explained the circumstances already known to our readers. " I am in a sorry plight, Sir Edward," continued our hero, with a smile, and casting a look at his certainly much the worse for wear and tear, uniform, " I lost everything in the Droits."

" It matters not what a brave man has on, when he has a clear conscience, Mr. Chamberlain; and, by Jove! your prizes will rig you out in style. Pray make no apologies for your rough appearance." So saying, Sir Edward led the way to the cabin.

During dinner the conversation was not confined to any particular topic; but when the things were removed, and the wine circulated, Sir Edward expressed a wish to know how a midshipman of the Leander came to be a prisoner on board the Droits.

Though our hero was very willing to give a brief recital of his adventures, he nevertheless felt disinclined to mention particulars respecting Miss Mortimer, and also what had occurred to himself during his short stay in the chateau de Hauteville; suppressing therefore all mention of Annie Mortimer, he gave Sir Edward a very fair and candid account of his shipwreck and escape, and his action with the privateer.

CHAPTER II.

Sir Edward Pellew listened with great attention and indeed interest to our hero's account of himself, and when he finished the worthy and gallant commander of the Indefatigable said, with a pleased smile,

" I congratulate you, Mr. Chamberlain, not only on your exceeding good fortune in getting out of your very perilous situation, but on the gallant conduct with which you followed up your good luck. Now I think I can render you a service that will benefit and please you, as well as enabling you to be of service to your country.

" Lord Bridport is off Brest at this moment

c 2

with several large ships. Your prize, the Belle
Poule, is a notorious privateer, and said to be
one of the fastest out of the French ports, the
cutter you so gallantly and singularly captured,
you can send with everything of value you
have in the schooner to Plymouth; there is no
fear of her being retaken, for we have made a
clean sweep of the channel. How many men
have you altogether?"

"I can count sixteen, Sir Edward, all able
and willing hands."

Sir Edward Pellew smiled, and, turning to
his first lieutenant, said, "it's a true adage,
fortune favours the brave."

"Ah," returned Leiutenant Spencer, "there's
not a doubt of that, Sir Edward; but no one
can deny but that the fickle jade has
favourites."

The baronet laughed. "You must, Mr.
Chamberlain, accompany me with your
schooner till we join Lord Bridport. It so
happens that we have not a single small vessel
with the fleet, and our admiral wants to send

important information to Sir John Jervis, who is now in Lisbon. Your schooner is a very fast craft. I will put on board a dozen good men, and you will make the best of your way to Lisbon. You must assume the rank of lieutenant, and your schooner will probably be made a tender to your old ship the Leander, which is now in the Mediterranean. Is there any trustworthy seaman on board capable of taking charge of the cutter to Plymouth ?"

" Yes, Sir Edward, a Mr. Hawkins, who was first mate of the Fox privateer, a good seaman, and a highly respectable man."

" Very good," returned Sir Edward. " You had now better return on board your ship. It was a mere chance my being so near you to-day. My consorts are watching the French fleet shut up in Brest. I made a stretch to sight the Penmarks, to see if any of our ships were cruising off Belle Isle."

After some further instructions from Sir Edward, our hero retired, returning the kind-hearted commander thanks for the interest he evinced in his welfare.

As Augustus Chamberlain was pulled back to the Belle Poule, he was thinking how he could manage respecting the Mortimers. It would be some time before he could reach England. As for the service he was required to perform, it was a most important step for him. He would have the rank of lieutenant, and afterwards be appointed, with his schooner, as a tender to the Leander—a most pleasing species of service for a young and enterprising officer. After due reflection, he made up his mind to write full particulars of the Mortimer family to Mr. Calthurst, their confidential agent, who alone could act with any prospect of success to rescue them from captivity.

The conduct of Monsieur de Hauteville sorely perplexed and troubled him. What could he mean or intend by such treachery towards him? Could he have any designs on Annie Mortimer? This thought drove the hot blood to his cheek. Still, as far as he was concerned, he was powerless to act; on Mr. Calthurst, therefore, everything depended.

On reaching the schooner, he had her brought close to the cutter, and sent for Mr. Hawkins, and explained all to him, and that he intended him to take the cutter to England, and hand her over, with all her valuables, to the proper authorities, except the sum of two thousand pounds belonging to Mrs. Penson, which he would restore to her. " I shall not be in England myself for a month, I dare say, so let us arrange how we may meet when I do return. I have a most important letter to write, and must depend on your delivering it in person to the gentleman to whom it is addressed."

" You may depend upon me, Mr Chamberlain. I sincerely regret I am not going with you. Promise me, if it should be in your power," and he looked earnestly into the lieutenant's face, " if it be in your power, and you are appointed with the schooner as tender to the Leander, that you will give me a berth. I don't care if it's one before the mast, so that I sail with you."

The person addressed held out his hand, and pressed the mate's warmly.

"All I can say, Mr. Hawkins, is that I will not sail without you. I know the benefit such a friend and so good a seaman would be to me, and will avail myself eagerly of your offer of service."

"Then," said the mate, with a joyful rubbing of the hands, "please God, we will make this little schooner spoken of before the war ends, if our lives are spared."

Our hero descended into the cabin and told Mrs. Penson and Rose of the new order of things. Rose looked sad. "Mr. Hawkins," she said, "is a kind, brave man, and we will willingly trust our lives to his care; but we shall feel your loss, Augustus, and God knows when we may meet again."

"Not many weeks hence, I hope, Rose," replied our hero. "Where, Mrs. Penson, shall I find you and Rose when I return?"

" You will always hear of us, my dear boy, at the little cottage at Chelsea, on the banks of the Thames. That cottage will, most likely, be my home when I am able to travel there."

" Ah," said Rose, looking affectionately at our hero, " Do you remember the many happy little trips on the river we used to take when we were children, with old Jim, the waterman, with his wooden leg; and all the stories—yarns he called them—he used to tell us."

" They were happy days, Rose," said the lieutenant, thoughtfully; " life has opened on us both since then. I doubt if we shall ever feel as light of heart as then."

" I shall not," said Rose, somewhat sadly; "God grant that you may. But what will you do about Miss Mortimer, so young and so lovely, amongst strangers and enemies. She may remain a captive for months, perhaps years."

" I hope not, Rose. No exertion or money will be spared by her father's agent to effect an exchange or ransom. I am going to write

c 5

a long letter to him to-night, to send by Mr. Hawkins. We shall not part company till to-morrow, as our course lies the same way. I have not had ten minutes' conversation with him. He knows nothing of the adventures I so briefly told you after my shipwreck in the seventy-four; but I trust we shall be companions for many a long day after this mission of mine to Lisbon is over."

"A better man never lived," said Mrs. Penson. "He is much younger than my dear husband was, and they were like brothers. He has seen many strange scenes in foreign parts, and is, though only a mate, a very well-educated man, and very respectably connected. His father was once a very well-to-do merchant, and owned several fine ships."

Before sunset Mrs. Penson and Rose were put on board the cutter. By that time the sailors had made a temporary mast-head on the splintered mast, and were able to hoist the mainsail, with two reefs tied down.

A gun, fired from the Indefatigable, boomed

over the sparkling waters. It was a glorious sunset—sea and sky, purple and gold, mingling together. The lofty sails of the frigate remained tinged with the light after the orb of light had sunk beneath the wave; and the three vessels, with all sail set, stood away for the north-east—the frigate, however, reducing her canvas as night set in, so as not to outrun the Belle Poule; but, in the breeze then blowing, the schooner could hold her own easily with the Indefatigable; but she also slacked sail, to allow the cutter to keep company.

Augustus Chamberlain spent several hours in writing to Mr. Calthurst the full particulars of the wreck of the Droits, and the consequences of that fearful disaster upon the Mortimer family. He stated where Miss Mortimer was—under the care of a French gentleman of the name of Hauteville; was minute in every particular, and implored Mr. Calthurst to spare neither exertion nor funds to expedite her release.

The bright and glorious sunset was a type of life—for before midnight a dense fog fell over the waters, and the breeze freshened into the south-east. Tom Darking came into the cabin before our hero had finished writing.

" There's a shift of wind, sir, and a dense fog has come off the land."

" Where did you see the cutter, Tom?"

" She was about three miles astern, sir, before the fog came on. I think some of the rigging slipped from the mast-head, for we saw them lower the mainsail, and a couple of men went aloft. Bill Barker could see them through the glass."

" I hope the fog will blow off, Tom. I should not wish to miss the cutter, though this is the season of fog off this coast. How is our head?"

" Nearly nor'-west, sir. We could see the frigate's lights when the fog first came on; but now we can't see our foremast."

" A nor'-west will clear all the rocks and

shoals off the Somme," said our hero.
"When I have finished writing I will come
upon deck. Who is at the wheel?"

"Bill Barker, sir."

An hour afterwards the young lieutenant
was on deck. The change in the weather
was singular—it was piercing cold, a dense
fog, and with every prospect of a blow-out
from the east and south.

"This fog is very provoking, Bill," said
the lieutenant to the old tar.

"Why yes, sir—I hates 'em, myself. I'd
rather anyday a treble-reefed mainsail than
this here nasty fog. With the best look-out
and reckoning a man does not always hit his
course; besides the chance of being run into
by some lubber, who never keeps his weather-
eye open, clear or thick. Nor'-west will clear
all, sir, won't it?"

"Yes, and plenty to spare," said the lieutenant, "the frigate will give the reefs a
wider berth. Just burn a blue light till we

see if either the frigate or the cutter will see and answer it."

There was a large case of various lights and night signals on board, and in a moment its vivid blue shed a faint light through the thick vapour. In less than five minutes the signal was answered seaward.

"That's from the frigate," said our hero. "She must be very close indeed. I fear the cutter is considerably astern; however, at sunrise this fog may disperse."

The schooner was put under easy sail, and our hero, though rather uneasy, retired for a couple of hours' rest. He was again on deck before the dawn made. The breeze had considerably slackened. and as it lulled, the fog lay more dense upon the heaving waters.

"This is certainly unfortunate," thought the young man. Just at that moment the dull boom of a large gun was heard to windward.

"That's the frigate again, sir," said Tom Darking, who was steering.

"She is about four miles off," replied our hero; "fire our gun in reply."

This was done, but no response came from where they supposed the cutter might be, if she had steered the same course as themselves. The day passed without any change; but as the watch was set for the night it came on to rain a thick, drizzly, continuous fall, and before morning it changed to snow and sleet, the wind in the north-east blowing half a gale.

"Well," thought our hero, "one cannot complain of want of variety." The breeze increased, and the snow began to fall heavily. A most careful watch was kept, for their situation was rather critical. According to Lieutenant Chamberlain's reckoning they ought to be some few miles off the tremendous range of rocks and banks that cause the rapid race of Fontenead and in the direct line of ships leaving the port of Brest and steering for the westward. About an hour after midday the entire crew came on deck, when the clear sound of a very large ship's bell was distinctly heard, evidently not five hundred yards to windward.

" Put her about, my lads," said the lieutenant, running to the wheel, " that bell is from a large ship, and we are right in her course if she is going dead before the wind."

In an instant the schooner was in stays, and hardly paid-off and gathered way, before a huge ship loomed through the driving snow. The hull was seen for a moment, as it flitted by—a man in the chains calling out the depth of water in French.

" By Jove!" exclaimed our hero, drawing his breath. " A providential escape—that was a French two-decker."

For an instant the men were stupified, so fearfully close did the two-decker shave the schooner.

About four o'clock it began to cease snowing, and before sunset the sky rapidly cleared to the north, with a fine fresh breeze. Anxiously our hero scanned the horizon all round. About four miles astern of him, to leeward, was the Indefatigable, lying to under double-reefed topsails; and some eight or nine miles to windward were four large men-of-war, under easy sail. The land was distinctly visible about ten miles to the eastward; but nowhere was there any vessel resembling the Sans Pareil.

"No doubt," said our hero, "the cutter has stood out to sea, and will make for the English coast. With her crippled mast, it was dangerous for her to remain near the land, and so short, too, as she is in hands."

"Aye, aye, sir," returned Bill Barker, "that was her wisest course, for any small armed lugger from the land might capture her."

Our hero bitterly reproached himself for not having written the letter on board the cutter, and given it to Mr. Hawkins before parting.

All on board were watching the Indefatigable, which now began to make sail, and lie

up for the Belle Poule—and then both together worked up to where the four large
British ships-of-war were watching the port
of Brest.   Our hero at once guessed the
French two-decker that passed him had taken
advantage of the snow storm to slip her
moorings, and run to sea. When close enough
to the frigate, the latter lay to, and immediately lowered a boat, which, with four hands,
pulled alongside the Belle Poule.   There was
a midshipman steering, and on coming alongside, he said—

" Sir Edward's compliments—he wishes to
see you aboard, sir," addressing the lieutenant.

" Very good," replied our hero, stepping
into the gig, " I am at his command."

" Did any ship pass you, Mr. Chamberlain,
during the last twenty-four hours," enquired
the young middy ; a fine lad, not more than
fifteen years old.

" Yes," returned our hero, " and very nearly
went over us.   It was a French two-decker."

"Ah, by Jove, the old quarter-master was right—but here we are."

Chamberlain sprung up the steps, and stood upon the deck.

" Upon my word, Mr. Chamberlain," said one of the lieutenants, " that craft of yours works beautifully ; you have not lost any time lying to in the snow storm."

" No, sir; I kept working to windward." Just then, they joined Sir Edward on the quarter deck.

" Dirty weather these last three days, Mr. Chamberlain," said Sir Edward, after kindly receiving our hero. " I was rather uneasy about you ; yesterday, Quarter-master Campbell declared that a large ship passed us, going dead before the wind, in the height of the snow storm. Now I know old Campbell is a remarkably sharp hand, and as keen sighted a customer as you would meet in the Highlands of Scotland, gifted with second sight. Still, as no one else saw anything of the kind, I doubted the accuracy of either his vision or hearing."

" A French two-decker, Sir Edward, very nearly went over me yesterday; had I not gone in stays on hearing the bell, the Belle Poule's days would have been numbered."

"God bless me, that's strange," said the Baronet, turning to his first lieutenant, " I think the old man must be gifted with second sight. You cannot be mistaken, Mr. Chamberlain, at all events."

" No, Sir Edward, I cannot, for I distinctly saw her hull, and heard the man in the chains give out thirty fathoms, in French."

" That's the way they do, Sir Edward," said the lieutenant, " a fair starting breeze, and a snow storm, and they slip through our fingers."

" Do you require any repairs, Mr. Chamberlain, to the schooner?" enquired Sir Edward.

" A couple of carpenters, and a little paint, Sir Edward, would do all required in a few hours."

"Well, you shall have all you wish, and be provisioned before this time to-morrow ; and you shall have your dispatches. Yonder are some of the ships of Lord Bridport's fleet. The leading ship is the Royal George ; she carries the admiral's flag, so now you can return, and keep close up with me."

Returning Sir Edward Pellew his warm thanks for his kindness and patronage, our hero returned to the Belle Poule, leaving his letter on board the Indefatigable to be forwarded to England by the first vessel from the fleet proceeding there.

We may here state that his letter, through a most untoward accident, never reached its destination; they, and nearly a hundred others, being accidentally destroyed four days afterwards by fire

Before sunset the following day, the Belle Poule was completely repaired, and stored with provisions and ammunition. The dispatches for Sir John Jervis, delivered to our hero in a sealed bag, with instructions to sink it if overpowered or pursued by the enemy, and his chance of escape hopeless. Fourteen additional men, and a smart midshipman, a young gentleman of the name of Mc Donald, from Ireland, were added to his crew ; he received also his commission as lieutenant from Lord Bridport himself, and thus prepared for every contingency, the Belle Poule left the fleet, with a steady favourable breeze, on her voyage to Lisbon.

CHAPTER III.

Augustus Chamberlain and Monsieur de Hauteville parted on the hill leading down to the little quay, where the Fraternity lugger lay at anchor, the former to go on board the vessel, whilst the latter retraced his way slowly towards the chateau. When he came upon the main road, which was crossed by another road leading to the battery of Pierre Point, he paused, for, advancing towards him, he caught sight, in the faint light, of the figure of a man; this figure soon stood beside him.

" Ah, Captain Popatin, are you out to see how our project works?"

"Oui, monsieur," returned the captain, "I was exceedingly anxious, fearing some contre-temps might occur."

"Well, there is only one mistake made, which I only recollected, when too late to remedy it."

"Diable! and what is that, monsieur?" enquired the captain.

"Why, I forgot to take a large blunderbuss and two heavy cutlasses I had in the lugger away with me. Now, if old François, who is as watchful as a cat, hears them getting into the lugger, he is sure to kill one or other with the blunderbuss."

"Sans doute," returned the captain, rubbing his hands, "if he does, it will save Captain le Mery, of the Sans Pareil, any further trouble; and you, monsieur, would be certain that there was an end of that troublesome garçon Anglais."

"You quite mistake my intention, Monsieur Popatin," said De Hauteville, angrily. "I do not wish the young man any personal injury;

he is a brave youth, and I admire him. All I required was to place him in a situation from whence he could not extricate himself, for many months, perhaps till the cessation of the war. As a prisoner, caught in attempting to escape, he would be strictly confined, and neither allowed to be exchanged nor ransomed. But to have him killed by old François was very foreign to my intention."

" Mille pardons, monsieur," returned the captain, humbly, " as yet no such accident has occurred, or we should have heard the report of the gun, and ere this they must have put to sea in the lugger."

" Let us walk back to the beach," said De Hauteville, " and satisfy ourselves of the fact."

And turning back, the two ill-assorted companions in a wicked project proceeded towards the descent to the beach.

"You are quite sure, Popatin, that Captain le Mery received my letter in good time ?

" Quite sure, monsieur. For his answer to

me was that he would watch the channel to the north closely, and it is not at all likely that the runaways would make sail to the southward."

"No, I should say not," returned De Hauteville thoughtfully. "Hark! did you hear that shout?"

"Diable!" returned Popatin, "there is some one shouting fiercely down on the beach."

"Then, all's right," said De Hauteville. "They have secured François and his comrade, and put them in the shed. Let them bide, they will do right well there till morning. You can go back, Popatin, to the battery, and this day month you may expect your captain's commission and appointment to a more important station. Not impossible, but I may get you made commandant of Louvain. You would then be quite close to my chateau d'Auray, where Madame de Morni is now residing, and there you may be of service to me hereafter."

"I am devoted to your interests, Monsieur de Hauteville," returned the would be captain and future commandant of Louvain, a rather important castle and fort on the entrance to the Varrenes estuary.

" Well, good night, Popatin," said De Hauteville ; "bring me the earliest intelligence of the captain of the Fraternity, for I shall be anxious to hear."

" We shall not hear before Thursday, Monsieur, as the Sans Pareil is bound for Vannes, whither she will take her prize. It is reported that an English fleet of fifteen sail of the line is off Brest. So she will not attempt that port."

The confederates separated. Monsieur de Hauteville returned to the chateau, and quietly retired to his apartment.

Before he had left his chamber the next morning there was a commotion in the chateau. The two guardians of the lugger Fraternity had been released by some peasants going to their work, and had instantly started for the chateau, with the terrible intelligence that a party of English had landed in boats, and after a desperate struggle had carried off the lugger and left them tied hand and foot.

Then came the news from Pierre Point Battery that three English prisoners had broken out of the prison and escaped.

By the time Monsieur de Hauteville had dressed, a great crowd of the peasantry, all armed with various agricultural implements, were assembled to repel an invasion by the sacre Anglais.

Monsieur de Hauteville quietly dismissed them, saying he was happy to see their readiness to repel a landing of the perfidious English; but the fact was that the captives at Pierre Point battery had broken out of prison and seized his lugger, Fraternity, and put to sea. But he had no doubt they would be captured again, and confined in a more secure prison. He then ordered the peasants an allowance of wine, who, having drank to the

health of their gracious master, shortly afterwards departed to their several occupations,
quite confident that their individual valour
was quite able to drive any marauding English
into the sea.

When Mademoiselle de Morni entered the
breakfast saloon, Monsieur de Hauteville was
standing before a blazing log fire, reading a
despatch he had just received from Paris.

Eugenie saluted her uncle, who returned
her salutation, kindly, saying without raising
his head from the paper—

" I suppose the row made here this morning disturbed you. You have heard, of course,
by this time, of the escape of our prisoner,
Monsieur Chamberlain, with three other Eng-
lishmen from the fort."

" Yes," returned Eugenie, quietly pouring
out a cup of coffee. " They managed it exceedingly clever. They have got off, I
suppose, taking with them your pretty little
lugger."

Monsieur de Hauteville glanced over the
paper he was reading, and looked into the
calm, unconcerned features of his niece. She
appeared not the least interested or disturbed,
but continued to pour out her coffee, and to
commence her breakfast with alacrity.

" They certainly did," continued her uncle,
folding up his despatch, and sitting down to
the table, " but I do not think they will get
far out to sea, for Popatin has sent me word
that the Sans Pariel was all last night
in our bay, and no doubt will recapture the
' Fraternity.' "

" I hope not," said Eugenie, " I do not see
what good it would do us, or la belle France,
to retain three or four poor fellows captives for months, perhaps years."

" Very true, ma chere," returned De Hauteville, breaking a turkey's egg. " How is
Mademoiselle Mortimer? Did she hear the
uproar those valiant fellows made early this
morning? Old François swears that there

were twenty English who boarded the lugger. He had a loaded blunderbuss with him, but, in his haste, forgot all about it."

"Lucky for him he did," said Eugenie, seriously, "or he might, in his fright, have fired it, and killed some one."

De Hauteville laughed, saying, "I see, Eugenie, you have no great opinion of my coxswain's valour; but tell me, how is our patient?"

"Infinitely better, and the intelligence of Monsieur Chamberlain's escape has inspired her with courage, and raised a feeling of hope in her breast."

"You must still keep the intelligence of her mother's unfortunate death a secret," said Monsieur de Hauteville. "Let her get strong before we venture to tell her anything so sad. We shall have news this evening from Brest, and perhaps learn whether her father was rescued from the wreck or not. It would be a fearful blow, the loss of both parents." After a moment's pause he con-

tinued, " She would then be heiress to half-a
million of money. What a fortune! Par
Dieu! those English are wonderful people
for making money."

"I dare say," said Eugenie, sadly, " that
the poor girl would willingly, if she had the
power, give the half-million you speak of, to
be restored to the embraces of her parents,
and alas! I have a presentiment she has lost
them both."

"She is very young," said Monsieur de
Hauteville, " but youth readily forgets, hap-
pily so. Change of scene, care and attention,
and the gratification of every wish, will wean
her mind from the past. I will spare no
pains. no expense, to make her happy."

" And you will utterly fail," said Mademoiselle de Morni seriously and sadly,
looking her uncle steadily in the face, " You
quite misjudge this girl's character; young
as she is, the feelings of her heart are
deep scated, and not to be easily rooted
out or turned into another channel. Time

will, of course, soften the agony and distraction she will feel when she learns the loss of her parents ; though scarcely sixteen, she loves with a fervour and devotion, and also with a confidence that neither time nor suffering will ever break."

" Bah !" exclaimed De Hauteville, with an angry flush spreading over cheek and forehead, " this is all romance and delusion. I know better. What! a childish attachment of some months, perhaps a year, to gain such a hold as you imagine. My dear Eugenie," he added, with a smile, " women are poor judges of their own sex's feelings ; two years hence you will talk differently."

" And do you think," said Mademoiselle de Morni, " that no enquiry will be made after this young girl—the heiress of so much money—by the British government ?"

" She will be believed to have died," said De Hauteville. " If Monsieur Chamberlain reaches England, he left her exceedingly ill, as near death as possible. Who

will, or can, in the war that now rages
between the two countries, prove that she has
not died; and when she is my wife, my dear
niece, you will allow that it will be easy
to prove she did not die. Now, do not
let us argue this matter further; rest satisfied that I will work out the prophecy, on
the fulfilment of which rests the prosperity
and existence of the house of De Hauteville."

So saying, he left the saloon.

"Well!" mentally exclaimed Eugenie de
Morni, "what a strange and extraordinary
weakness and infatuation, nay superstition,
in a man, really generous and brave, and who
is considered, even by those in power, to
possess considerable attainments, too humane
in the ordinary affairs of life as to scarcely
crush a worm in his path, and yet to carry
out an insane idea, he actually plots to poison
and destroy the future happiness of two
young and noble-hearted creatures, devotedly
attached to each other. So blind is his faith
in the ravings of his old crack-brained grand-

mother, that he sinks and discards all the
finer feelings of his nature, and actually per-
suades himself that he is fulfilling a prophecy
he is bound to work out, and does not hesitate in employing any means to further his
plans ; I feel for him the strongest
affection, for did he not peril life a dozen
times to rescue my beloved mother and myself from a horrible doom, and yet I must
try to defeat his projects, and rescue this
poor girl from a life of constant repining
and bitterness."

Thus soliloquising, Eugenie de Morni
arose, and opening the glass doors leading
into the garden, walked out. The morning
was cold, the wind blowing fresh, and the
sky leaden and overcast; the breeze
whistled through the trees, and rustled the
decayed leaves on the well-gravelled walks.
There was nothing inviting, either in the
aspect of the weather, or the look of the garden to tempt out-door exercise, for at times
a slight drizzle was borne along on the

wintry blast; but, nevertheless, Eugenie,
who had put on her bonnet, and wrapped herself in a large warm shawl, closing the glass
doors, proceeded along the gravel walk till
she arrived at the gate opening into the path
that led to the main road. S'..e came out
on the road, and along it she walked at a
quick pace, for nearly a mile. She then
ascended the hill, from whence a view of the
sea was to be had, and near the summit she
beheld a man, wrapped in a thick woollen
coat, such as French pilots wear even at the
present day. The man, as he reached the
side of Mademoiselle de Morni, took off his
fur cap, and saluted very humbly. He was past
middle age, but hale and strong, with a good,
sunburnt countenance, and hands large and
bony, of the colour of tanned leather. He
had fisher.nan's high boots on, and carried a
shrimping pole and net on his shoulder. This
fisherman, pilot, and shrimper, was the brother of Madame Morelle, the housekeeper at
the Chateau de Hauteville.

THE NAVAL LIEUTENANT. 61

"Well, François," said mademoiselle, "you performed your part this morning admirably. I hope you did not suffer much by being tied hand and foot for so many hours."

"Ah! pardieu, mademoiselle," returned the fisherman, with a quiet smile, "they tied us, I can tell you, rather tightly. I did not mind it; but my comrade, André, shouted lustily though I told him he was wasting his breath."

"Do you think the young Englishman thoroughly understood your directions, and that he will follow them?"

"Ah, ma foi, mademoiselle. No doubt of it. He speaks French like a native; besides, he's a sailor; therefore no fear of his misunderstanding my plain sailing directions"

"Did he seem surprised at your knowledge of his intention to escape in the lugger, or did he ask any questions?"

"Surprised he was, mademoiselle; but in a moment he recovered himself, saying, as he squeezed my hand; and, ma foi, he has a grasp like a vice, 'I will do as you direct,

mon ami.   I will not ask you any questions,
because it would be indiscreet, but this service will never be forgotten, and one day I
may repay *you*, at all events.' "

" Ah! " said Eugenie, with an additional
colour in her cheek. " He—but no matter,
François—you did your part right well, and
here's your reward," and the French girl
dropped ten gold pieces into the open palm
of the fisherman, who, with a very low bow,
conveyed it into an inner pouch in his
woollen coat.

" Now, François, I expect you will try and
find out whether the lugger escaped the cutter;
that's all, of course, we can expect to learn.
You have shown your gratitude for the kindness you received when a prisoner in England.
You have returned the compliment. An
Englishman gave you freedom, and you have
given one, indeed, four of his countrymen
a chance of freedom. Now, farewell, I shall
find means to see you again; but do not you
seek to see me."

" Many thanks, mademoiselle, for your generosity. I accept what you so generously
give me; but, ma foi, I say it without
boasting, I would have acted as you desired
me without hope of reward."

Mademoiselle de Morni smiled, and bidding
the worthy fisherman good bye returned to the
chateau.

An hour later, Eugenie de Morni was sitting beside the cheerful log fire in the inva-
lid's chamber. Annie Mortimer in health
was much better ; she was sitting opposite the
kind-hearted Eugenie in a large easy-chair,
looking exceedingly thin and pale, but her
voice was stronger, and her eyes seemed less
sunken in the head.

" I am sure, mademoiselle," said Annie, in
reply to a remark of Eugenie's, " I can never
be sufficiently thankful and grateful to you
and to Monsieur de Hauteville, for the extraordinary generosity evinced towards me; but
for you, I should have perished; the greatest
attention and kindness could alone have re-

stored me, knowing as I do from the prompt-
ings of my heart, that I am an orphan—
fatherless and motherless. It is useless, mademoiselle, to disguise the fatal intelligence; I
have felt from the very first that such was
God's will."

" But, indeed, mademoiselle," said Eugenie de Morni; " as I said, no positive intelligence has reached us respecting your
father—there is still hope."

" Alas! no," returned Annie, " for even as
we quitted that fatal and doomed ship life was
nearly extinct with him."

Bending her head upon her hands, Annie
Mortimer remained buried in the profound
misery of her own heart. In a few days a
visible improvement took place in her health.
The intelligence of Mr. Mortimer's death and
burial at Brest reached the chateau, and
Eugenie de Morni felt relieved that Annie
had anticipated this melancholy event.

Monsieur de Hauteville suddenly set out
for Paris, telling his niece that the moment

he returned he should take her and
Mademoiselle Mortimer to Auray, where
Madame de Morni had preceded them to see
that the chateau was put in order.

A good deal of excitement existed in the
vicinity of Chateau de Hauteville on account
of the escape of the four English prisoners,
and the seizure of the lugger Fraternity.
But the intelligence brought to the chateau
some days after the escape of the prisoners
quite electrified the inhabitants of the chateau,
its hamlets, and the garrison of Pierre Point.
Two sailors, natives of Audierne had returned
to their homes ; who had formed part of the
crew of the Sans Pareil cutter. They gave
an account of their being captured, after a
desperate fight, by a party of English sailors,
who had surprised and taken the Belle Poule
privateer, and that these English sailors were
the very prisoners who had escaped from
Captan Popatin's battery, and seized the
lugger Fraternity, which vessel they sunk by

firing into her during the fight between the
Belle Poule and the Sans Pareil.

François was in a state of intense excitement
whilst relating the above particulars to Mademoiselle de Morni, who also listened to this apparently wonderful statement with considerable astonishment.

"But, François," said Eugenie, "all this
is incredible; four prisoners, without arms,
could not take a privateer with twenty-five
in her; besides the Belle Poule is re-
nowned on this coast for her daring and the
success of her enterprises."

"Ma foi, mademoiselle," returned the bewildered fisherman, "so I said; but you see
there's no possibility of disbelieving the two
sailors; the whole crew of the Sans Pareil
were allowed to go ashore in their boats,
by the young captain of the Belle Poule;
they landed to leeward of the Penmarks and
are gone on to Brest, all except these two
who are slightly wounded, and who came

to their native place, to get completely cured."

"You may depend on it, François," said Mademoiselle de Morni, "that there were more English than our four escaped prisoners, wherever they came from. Just go over to Audierne yourself, and see the two sailors. I should like to hear the full particulars. There are five francs to bear your expenses."

"I will go, mademoiselle, this moment, and be back to-morrow morning, when you shall have true information."

Miss Mortimer was by this time able to leave her room; sad and resigned, the young girl's entire thoughts rested upon the sad events that had deprived her of her dearly-loved parents, and of Augustus—had he succeeded in getting to England, and would he be able to get her restored to her country?

She shuddered when she thought how desolate and friendless she should be, even when restored to freedom. Her young life would be passed among total strangers. Already she had begun to love the kind hearted and generous Eugenie de Morni, and to feel that to be deprived of her affectionate attention and kindness would be a renewal of her feelings of desolation and utterly friendless state. She never for an instant doubted the love and devotion of Augustus, but she was not so young as not to know that at the moment she set foot on British soil she would become either a ward in chancery, or be placed under the guardianship of strangers, for relations she knew of none. Consequently any close intercourse with her youthful lover would be strictly forbidden.

As she sat in the evening near a blazing wood fire, in one of the comfortable small saloons of the chateau, where Mademoiselle de Morni usually passed her time, Eugenie informed her of the strange tidings brought to the chateau by old François, the fisherman.

Annie listened with eager attention. Her

large, lustrous eyes, fixed on the French demoiselle's expressive features.

" Ah ! " she exclaimed, " I always thought Augustus was born to do brave and gallant actions. His very nature is so true and generous—he has no fear in his disposition, and yet he is as gentle and as kind as one of our own sex. And so he has not only escaped, but also fought and taken a privateer and a French cruiser ? "

" So it appears, Annie," said Eugenie, looking with admiration into the beautiful face of her companion, and thinking how very lovely that face would be when health and happiness, for a year or two would have driven away all traces of past sorrows, and softened down the memory of her cruel bereavement. Annie had repeatedly asked would it not be possible that Monsieur de Hauteville could take her to the spot where her beloved mother's remains lay interred. An intense desire to visit her grave had taken possession of her mind, and Eugenie had

promised to exert her influence with her
uncle, as soon as her health became sufficiently restored to take the journey to
Quimper.

When positive information of the death of
Mr. Mortimer reached the Chateau de Hauteville, and Mademoiselle de Morni communicated the sad intelligence to Annie, it
occasioned no increased shock to her feelings;
but the grief it created in her sensitive heart
was long and deep. She gave way to no
violent burst of weeping; but she sorrowed
much, and in secret wept over the sad fate of
both her parents.

Time rolled on—two months passed over,
and Annie Mortimer was able to take
exercise in the open air; and, when fine, she
and Eugenie visited many of the relics of
past ages in which Bretagne abounds, and
near to the Chateau de Hauteville. Naturally
cheerful, and very conversable and exceedingly well-educated Miss Mortimer, for one
so young, was a most endearing companion.

Though her cheerfulness no longer existed,
she still exerted herself to be a companion
to the amiable, kind-hearted girl, who studied
to relieve her mind, and occupy her thoughts ;
they, therefore, soon learned to love each
other, and when, at the expiration of nearly
three months, Monsieur de Hauteville returned from Paris, and escorted his niece and
Annie during one of their rambles in the
vicinity of the chateau, he was powerfully
struck, and even excited, by the wonderful
change in the person and appearance of the
latter. Alighting from his horse, and throwing the bridle to a groom, Monsieur de
Hauteville walked to the chateau by the side
of the two fair and beautiful girls—one his
niece, the other, in his own mind, his intended bride.

Monsieur de Hauteville, we have said, was
a tall, handsome man, still in the prime of
life, of insinuating manners, and extensively
acquainted with all the antiquities and
legends of Brittany. After the first few

words of greeting, and kind enquiries after
Miss Mortimer's health, and gentle hints of
how vastly improved she was in appearance,
seeing the colour vary in the cheek of the
English maiden, he adroitly turned the conversation upon the singular and remarkable
Druidical remains they had just left when he
overtook them on the road; and in his easy,
quiet way gave them a very clear and lucid
account of the Druidical remains in the
vicinity of de Hauteville, which interested our
young heroine, and wore off that feeling of
unaccountable uneasiness which she had felt
when first they met Monsieur de Hauteville.
So that, by the time they reached the chateau,
Annie Mortimer felt less restraint in the
presence of Eugenie's uncle than she ever
thought she could experience.

The girls who slept in the same chamber
—it was their mutual wish—as soon as they
entered the house, retired to make some
change in their dress for dinner. When
alone Eugenie observed,

"Well, this uncle of mine has at last returned. We shall soon go to Castle Auray one of the loveliest spots in Brittany."

Annie sighed, and for the moment made no reply. So Eugenie, looking over to her friend, who was very serious, said, "Why do you sigh at mention of Chateau Auray?"

"Because, dear Eugenie, to go there will take me further from my never-to-be-forgotten mother's resting-place, and because—" she hesitated, and seeing her companion look anxious, she added, "because it appears to me as if some strange destiny was hanging over me, and that painful events will occur before I see my native land. It is not a dream, dearest, that agitates me; it is an unacccountable feeling—an overpowering sensation of uneasiness—I may say dread. It took possession of my mind, the first time my eyes rested on Monsieur de Hauteville. and I felt it again to-day when we met. His manner and his extreme kindness and generosity I can never forget; indeed, during our walk I felt this strange feeling abate; but still his presence oppresses me. Forgive me, my dear Eugenie—my more than sister—if I pain you by speaking thus of your kind uncle, to whom, next to Augustus, I may say I owe life, by his ordering me to be brought here, and confided to your love and attention. I should, undoubtedly, have sunk and died, had he not done as he did."

Eugenie de Morni thought seriously; but, after a moment, she looked up with a smile, saying, "Those kind of feelings are not altogether singular or unnatural; though, if we try to analyse them, we fail to satisfy ourselves. These melancholy ideas will pass away. We shall have news from England, when your gallant lover arrives there—you need not let that tell-tale cheek and fair brow of yours reveal your thoughts. You think you are too young to feel passion; but, dearest, it has taken deep root in your young heart. A tender fibre at first; but destined to grow and flourish, and hold possession of its first resting-place till it has gained a power that will conquer all. But come, be kind and unrestrained in my uncle's presence. He has many amiable qualities, and a kind and generous heart, though apt to give way to strange impulses. He is a firm believer in destiny, like his bosom friend, General Bonaparte, with whom he served in many a splendid campaign; and, I believe, now that this won-derful man is coming into power, that De Hauteville will again take part in this new and amazing change that has spread over France. But come to dinner. This evening I will give you a short account of my own personal adventures, and my share in the terrible scenes enacted in the ' Reign of Terror.' "

At dinner Monsieur de Hauteville paid great and hospitable attention to his fair young guest; but his manner and words were devoid of the slightest particular interest, except for her comfort. The conversation chiefly turned upon the strange scenes Mon-

sieur de Hauteville had witnessed in Paris—
his account of Bonaparte's appearance in the
council of five hundred, his terrible reception, and the manner in which his brother
Lucien won the applause of the nation by
dispersing the five hundred at the point of the
bayonet; and how, finally, before he left
Paris, Bonaparte had become undisputed
master of the noble empire of France.

"He is a wonderful man," remarked Eugenie, "I remember him well. When I saw
him about four years ago I little imagined
that he, the younger son of a decayed Corsican
family, insignificant in person, and by no
means otherwise attractive, could have at-
tained to such power."

"He is not on the last rung of the ladder
yet, Eugenie," said De Hauteville, "from a
consul he will step on to a throne. My
grandmother's prophecies begin to develop
themselves," and he cast a glance over the
thoughtful features of Annie Mortimer.

"But madame's prophecies," said Eugenie,

with a meaning look at her uncle, " end with
the downfall of the being, whoever that being
is, whom she, in her dreams, imagined gained
the summit of man's ambition."

" Such may be the case," returned de
Hauteville; " but, Mademoiselle Mortimer, I
am happy to say that there are rumours of
peace whispered amongst the politicians in
Paris."

" Oh!" exclaimed Miss Mortimer, " I trust
such rumours have their foundation in truth.
War, of which I know little, except in the
pages of history, must be a fearful scourge
to a people."

" Constituted as the world is, mademoiselle,"
said Monsieur de Hauteville, " war, though
an evil in itself, oftentimes brings beneficial
results. When France became convulsed—
her own children tearing her to pieces in the
name of liberty, the crowned tyrants of
Europe combined to crush her, and the liberty
she proclaimed: war then became inevitable.
France stood on the defensive—finally drove

back the legions that would have crushed
and annihilated her, and, under the glorious
banners of Bonaparte, has achieved her inde-
pendence, and completely humbled her would-
be oppressors. We have discovered that our
aspirations and enthusiasm for liberty were
a dream—an hallucination. We have placed
ourselves under the guidance of one head,
and that head will soon wear a crown.
Thus, singularly enough, we come back to
the point from whence we started. We de-
throned the Bourbon—we have waded through
rivers of blood to crush royalty, and enthrone
liberty—and, behold, we shall soon bow to
the symbol we swore to destroy for ever.
Such is man and his resolves. But to change
our subject," continued Monsieur de Hauteville,
"of course, mademoiselle, you have heard of the
gallant exploits of the young lieutenant, who
so cleverly managed to escape, and put to sea
in my little lugger, the Fraternity. Of course,
Eugenie, you contrived to glean all the particulars from old François," and Monsieur de

Hauteville looked very meaningly in the face of his niece.

"Oh, yes," returned Mademoiselle de Morni, quite unconcernedly, "François picked up the intelligence from the two wounded men belonging to the cutter Sans Pareil, who are natives of Audierne."

"No doubt his version of the story was quite correct. It is to be hoped, after so romantic an adventure, that your young friend, Monsieur Chamberlain," said De Hauteville, addressing our heroine, " contrived to follow up his good fortune, and has got to England— the most difficult part of the affair to accomplish, as our fleet had put to sea, and driven the English cruisers back to their own shores."

Annie Mortimer most devoutly hoped her lover had succeeded. She would not trust her voice with a reply, and Mademoiselle de Morni, seeing she was agitated, arose, and she and her young friend retired to their sitting room. It was yet day-light, for the gentry of

Brittany dined early, and as gentlemen in France did not sit over their wine, Monsieur de Hauteville, opening a cabinet, took out a folded document, which he put in his pocket, and taking his hat, left the chateau, and walked on towards the battery of Pierre Point.

It was the latter end of April—when the weather in that part of Brittany is charming—the trees were bursting with full foliage, and the hedge-rows were one mass of wild flowers. The country in the immediate vicinity of the chateau was well-cultivated. The terrors of the Revolution had ceased—the terrible Chouans, who some months back had carried terror into every cot, had been driven out of that part of Brittany by the skill and courage of De Hauteville, who, with a troop of chasseurs under his command, had cleared the country of those marauders, who vowed a terrible revenge, to which threat De Hauteville paid no attention.

As he approached the zig-zag path that led

from the sea beach to the battery of Pierre Point, he beheld Captain Popatin ascending, and he waited till that worthy reached his side. After saluting De Hauteville most humbly, the captain anxiously enquired how affairs were going on in Paris.

"Oh!" returned Monsieur de Hauteville, "You will have no reason to be dissatisfied, Captain Popatin," and taking out the folded paper he had put in his pocket, he handed it to the delighted commander of the four-gun battery, saying, "there is your captain's commission, and your appointment to —— Fort. You see I have kept my word, though, through some strange mischance, all our projects went wrong."

Captain Popatin bowed to the ground, and poured forth a torrent of words, with such strange gesticulations, that Monsieur de Hauteville laughingly interrupted him, saying he was quite satisfied that he had acted his part faithfully. "The only thing that puzzles me," continued de Hauteville, "is, why those

who escaped in the lugger should have steered
away to the southward, and made a run for
the Penmarks, when their course should have
taken them directly the reverse. I have been
to Brest, and seen the captain of the Sans
Pareil, who told me, when he first saw the
lugger she was under full sail, keeping along
the south shore, and making for the Penmarks; and that he should not have seen her
at all, only he happened to take a stretch to
the southward further than he intended during the night, it was so dark."

"Perhaps, monsieur," continued the captain of the Sans Pareil, "they considered the
weather too rough, and thought to run and
shelter under the Penmarks till it moderated.
The Fraternity was a small craft to cross the
Channel at such a time of the year."

"Now," said De Hauteville, thoughtfully,
"that idea is possible—however, they have
escaped. I did not wish the young man
harm; nevertheless, I must counteract the
consequences that may ensue. If enquiries

are made by relatives or friends, the young lady now in the chateau must be considered dead—that is for a time. You understand me ?"

"Oui, monsieur, I do ; if no personal investigation is made it will be easy to prepare a document to that effect, as the young lady could scarcely be said to be alive when washed ashore."

"Just so," said Monsieur de Hauteville, "and now it must be made clear that she died after the escape of the English prisoners. In a day or two she will leave this place for Auray. There will be no personal investigation during this war between the two nations—simply an enquiry. I shall want your signature to a paper I shall draw up, and also your brother's, the curé of St Colomb. He will have a better place shortly. So come up to the chateau in the evening, and I will have the paper ready."

"You shall be obeyed, monsieur," answered Captain Popatin. "You may depend on us."

" Very good. Recollect," added Monsieur
de Hauteville, " all this is for a temporary
purpose, and will be set right in time. No
one will suffer by it."

After some further conversation on other
subjects, Monsieur de Hauteville returned to
the chateau.

CHAPTER IV.

A FORTNIGHT passed without anything very remarkable occurring. Rumours were afloat of bands of brigands from La Vendée making excursions into Monsieur de Hauteville's district, and committing ravages, which roused De Hauteville to make enquiries into these rumours. After a good deal of investigation and trouble, and sundry excursions through the wild and extensive district lying south of the Chateau he discovered that these rumours had some foundation in truth. A mysterious band of thirty or forty men, well armed, had been seen in various places during several nights, but never during the day. He could not discern that any actual outrage had been committed on any farm, or that any chateau had been plundered. In fact, except having been seen after night-fall, and several shots having been distinctly heard by highly respectable farm-holders, De Hauteville would have considered this band of armed men a myth. He therefore contented himself by ordering a party of chasseurs quartered at Quimper to patrol the country where the band was said to have been seen several nights in succession; but nothing occurring to excite suspicion, this night-patrol ceased, and Monsieur de Hauteville prepared for transferring his household from Chateau de Hauteville to Castle Auray.

Miss Mortimer had daily improved in health since the spring commenced. The colour was coming back to her cheeks, but her former gaiety of spirit and buoyancy of heart was gone for a time. The fate of her parents was ever present to her mind, and the

only consolation she experienced was thinking of Augustus, and conjecturing how he
would act when he reached England. Young
as she was, she very well knew that a more
powerful feeling occupied her heart than
that of brotherly love for her young protec-
tor, and that feeling grew day by day stronger
and more deep-rooted—becoming the guiding
star of her existence.

Eugenie de Morni had received a letter
from her betrothed, a colonel in the army of
the gallant General Moreau, who had just obtained a brilliant victory over the Archduke
Charles, and was when he wrote the letter
about to march upon Vienna.

This letter from her long absent lover was
a delightful relief to the mind of the kind-
hearted Eugenie, who for a long time had
remained in suspense concerning the where-
abouts of one who was winning fame and re-
nown, under a general already so famous
amid the generals of the army of France.

Miss Mortimer could not but feel additional sadness, seeing the household all preparing for departure; to her this journey to Auray appeared to forebode a longer and wider separation from her native land, and to render her release and restoration to freedom more difficult; although Mademoiselle de Morni soothed her alarm, and endeavoured to prove to her that the change of residence could make no possible difference. Annie had also begun to fear that some mischance had occurred to Augustus. Three months had expired since his escape in the Fraternity, and no news of him, or intelligence from England. Surely, if he had reached England, steps would have at once been taken for her ransom or exchange.

To this reasoning Eugenie de Morni was troubled what to reply. She well knew that her uncle would defeat any negotiation set on foot—even her ingenuity was at fault, for she could not ascertain whether any enquiry had been instituted by Miss Mortimer's friends in England respecting her. Latterly, though

always considerate and kind, Monsieur de
Hauteville no longer made her a confidante
in his plans, or indeed spoke to her concerning his future intentions. Her mother was at
Chateau Auray waiting for them, so to Castle
Auray they must go. One slight piece of
intelligence she learned, which was that
Monsieur de Hauteville, in a month's time, was
to join Bonaparte in his intended campaign in
Italy and that he was to resume his rank of
general of division. Eugenie therefore thought
it would be very possible, during his absence,
to manage the escape of Miss Mortimer to
England, and this she resolved to attempt,
even at the risk of forfeiting her uncle's love
and protection.

Mademoiselle de Morni and our heroine
were to travel in one of the comfortable, but
somewhat ponderous Berlins of that period,
with their two female attendants, accompanied
by an escort of eight well-armed domestics.
Monsieur de Hauteville would follow in a few
hours on horseback. The journey would

only occupy two days; the first night they were to rest at a road-side auberge, which was exactly half-way; and to this inn relays of horses were sent, and domestics to have everything comfortably, and even elegantly arranged for them. The auberge De Bois Rouge was picturesquely situated, fronting a creek running up from the Gulf of Morbihan, and having at its back one of the most extensive woods in that part of France.

This auberge has been a favourite resort of aristocratic chasseurs in the days of the monarchy; and the house itself, a large and roomy building, was capable of affording excellent accommodation for noblemen, chasseurs, and their numerous attendants; but the Revolution had altered all this. Chasseurs there were none—the Chouans had driven all the gentry out of the country—and the auberge, though it still existed, was only the ghost of its former self. Few travellers frequented the road during those troublous times, so the once opulent landlord, his wife and two daughters, existed how they could, devoutly praying in secret for the good old days of the monarchy to return. Their only son had been taken away to the wars; but where he was, or whether alive or dead, they knew not.

The morning for departure arrived; Monsieur de Hauteville was most anxious that his treasured guest should travel with every comfort and safety. Two carriages contained all the females of the family, and the escort placed under the charge of his own special attendant, who had served several campaigns with him, and was a good and faithful attendant. It was a remarkably beautiful morning when our travellers started; Monsieur de Hauteville stating that he would be sure, if he did not overtake them before, to join them at supper at the Auberge de Bois Rouge.

" We look very formidable, my dear Annie," said Eugenie, with a smile, as the mounted and armed domestics divided, one half riding on before, the other following the two carriages.

" We certainly do," replied Miss Mortimer,
"but is there any danger expected, that we
should be so protected."

" I should say not," returned her friend,
" or my uncle would himself have formed one
of our escort; but, you see, we are like
generals, we move with our staff. There are
only two or three domestics at Castle Auray,
so we shall require our escort in other capa-
cities when we get there. I will not promise
you for most part of the way, from here to
Bois Rouge, either a pretty or a picturesque
country; but from the auberge to Auray,
you will pass through some lovely scenery."

Annie Mortimer, when seven years old, had
been taken to England by her mother, for the
benefit of her education; and in England she
had remained with her mother till she was
fourteen.

Her father had paid them two visits, of six
months each time.   On his last visit he took
them a most delightful excursion through
Devonshire and Dorsetshire before they all

returned to Barbadoes. Therefore she had
some idea, and some remembrance of both the
beauty of English scenery, and the delightful
travelling on English roads.

Now the roads in Brittany, even at the
present day, would try the endurance of not
only English springs, but those who trusted
their bodies to their support. But sixty-four
or sixty-five years ago, the roads through that
primitive, little-explored county, were literally
impassable to any carriage of English construc-
tion, even had it been one of Pickford's
waggons.

Suspended upon two immense leather braces,
the only springs, if you can misname them
springs, the heavy Berlin swayed from side
to side, then varied the motion by pitching
impetuously forward, whenever the drivers,
for there were two, one a postillion, the other
a coachman, were unlucky enough to drive
into an enormous rut, or rather pit, giving the
four heavy horses as much as they could do
to tug them out again. Annie was amazed

at the jerks and plunges the vehicle gave;
but Mademoiselle de Morni took them as
a matter of course, simply remarking, that
near Paris the roads were paved with great
square stones, which made the motion of a
carriage more agreeable; and then asking
Annie how they managed the roads in England, if they were worse or better, for as there
was much more rain in England than in
Brittany, the holes in the roads were no
doubt great pools of water.

Annie was unwilling to make odious com-
parisons, so she merely said that they took
great pains with the roads in England, and
had gates on them, charging for every carriage
and beast that passed a certain sum.

" Mon Dieu! how disagreeable," said the
French demoiselle, " to have to stop and pay
every moment. I suppose you carry a great
bag in a long journey, full of small money to
pay these gates. These joltings are good
exercise, and we are never required to stop."

At that moment, the right fore wheel disappeared into a monstrous hole full of water, throwing the carriage violently on one side, but not upsetting it. Eugenie burst into a merry laugh, as Miss Mortimer said, " there is one stop at all events, ma chere, and I do not think we shall get out of this hole in a hurry."

The four horses made prodigious efforts to drag the vehicle out, but snap went the traces and ropes, and the carriage became separated from the horses, the reins dragging the fat coachman into the pool, out of which he scrambled, uttering sundry maledictions against the postillion, on whom he laid the blame,the postillion returning the compliment, and having disengaged himself from a pair of boots certainly weighing not less than fifty pounds, he ran up to open the door of the voiture, whilst the attendants dismounted.

" Well, it's very clear we must get out," said Eugenie, laughing and requesting the two maids who sat on the front seat to lead the way. Having all four alighted, Eugenie and

our heroine said they would walk on whilst
they were mending the traces and releasing
the carriage. When this accident happened
they were within a league of Bois Rouge, and
the hour of the day about five o'clock.

Just as the two girls had reached the bank,
which was quite dry, and discovered a
pleasant path above the road, two horsemen
came up, and at once checked their steeds
close beside the path on which the ladies
stood. Eugenie de Morni and our heroine
naturally looked up into the faces of the
horsemen. One immediately dismounted,
threw the reins of his horse to his companion, and approaching, said, lifting his hat,
" I trust, ladies, that no one is hurt. Can
we be of any assistance?"

When she heard the stranger's voice, Annie
Mortimer gave a slight start, looking inquisi-
tively into the Frenchman's face. She appeared puzzled. The Frenchman was a tall,
strong-built man, perhaps two or three and
thirty, with dark hair and dark eyes, huge

whiskers, and bushy moustache. He wore a
kind of military undress suit of faded green.
He also regarded Miss Mortimer for a moment
with a fixed look ; but Mademoiselle Morni, in
answer to his question, at once said, " Thank
you. monsieur, we require no further help
than our attendants can afford us ; no one is
hurt," and with a slight inclination of her
head, passed on.

" Do you know, dear Annie, that you
started and changed colour when you first
saw that strange man. I do not call him
either an officer or a gentleman, notwithstanding his half-military dress. But, to return to what I was previously saying,
why did he startle you ?"

" In truth, my dear Eugenie, I can
scarcely account for my surprise. At the
moment I thought I had heard that voice
somewhere before, but that must be fancy.
Did you never hear a voice that struck you
as being heard before, and yet the person
speaking being a total stranger to you ?"

" Yes," returned Eugenie, with a shudder
her companion did not notice, " Once in my
life I did; some other time I will tell you on
what occasion. Ah! they have got our
voiture out of the pit, so there's an end of
our pleasant walk; but even this short exercise has been refreshing."

An hour afterwards they arrived before the
entrance to the Auberge Bois Rouge, and
several domestics ran out to assist their descent.

" What an immense rambling building,"
said Annie Mortimer, gazing at its quaint
gables, battlemented walls, and uneven roofs ;
its numerous ghost-like chimneys and oddly-
painted windows : a mass of antiquity, and a
monument of the eccentricity of builders, for
assuredly it must have had many architects.

" You are wondering, Annie, at the strange
looking building," said Mademoiselle de
Morni, as they crossed the wide court-yard,
" But if you are surprised at its exterior,
you will be indeed mystified at its interior.
You might wander for a day through its long

corridors and galleries, and perpetually find yourself returning to the same spot. I dare say there are nooks where the light of the glorious sun has not penetrated for a hundred years. Once I spent three days here, detained by fearful weather, and I used to explore all the grim hiding places it abounds with—winding staircases, that seem to conduct nowhere—old doors blocked up, leading you to fancy strange things behind them."

Just then the landlady made her appearance, looking, in truth, part and parcel of the strange building—she was quite as quaint in dress, and in manner; she was a relic of the past, and yet, in years, she numbered only sixty-five. She looked hale and active, and first embraced mademoiselle, kissing her on both cheeks, then doing the same to our heroine. After which making enquiries for Monsieur de Hauteville, she led the way to the best saloon, preceded by two attendants carrying antique candelabras, with four wax lights in each. The saloon was immense in its dimensions, and, although the month of May, a log fire blazed in the huge fire-place. In fact, the room, so long deserted, required fire to dispel the damp air that hung about everything in the old, deserted auberge.

"I hope, Dame Durand," said Mademoiselle de Morni, "that you have prepared the little blue chamber for our repose—we will occupy the same bed."

"Oui, mademoiselle," returned the land-lady, "I have had that chamber and three others well aired this whole week, so that you might have your choice. Will Monsieur de Hauteville be here to supper?"

She had scarcely said the words, when one of Monsieur de Hauteville's attendants entered the room, and handed Mademoiselle de Morni a sealed note, saying, "a horseman from the chateau, mademoiselle, has just arrived with this letter."

Eugenie de Morni broke the seal, and read the few lines it contained.

"Ah! Dame Durand, I can now answer your question. My uncle will not be here till three or four o'clock to-morrow, and he requests us to amuse ourselves here for one day as well as we can, as very pressing business detains him."

"Eh, bien, mademoiselle, I am very glad to have the honour and pleasure of your company for a day longer. I may then order your supper at once, for I am sure our roads must have given you an appetite."

"If they have not, dame, they at all events have shaken us well."

"Ah, ça! the roads are bad now, mademoiselle, for no one thinks it necessary to fill up the holes made by the winter rains; but from here to Auray you will find them much better."

The girls drew near to the blazing logs, feeling cold and lonely in the large cheerless looking apartment. Annie gazed wonderingly at its cumbrous, but once splendid decorations; the huge folds of its faded crimson curtains;

the lofty ceiling formerly representing some wonderful scene in heathen mythology; massive gilded cornices, antique mirrors, the once bright gilding now of a dingy brown, immense high-backed carved chairs, with velvet cushions, all spoke of past and faded grandeur.

" Surely," she observed to Eugenie, who appeared thoughtful, "this building, and this grand furniture did not always belong to an inn."

" Ma foi, no," said mademoiselle, rousing herself from her reverie, " this mansion and land, for leagues around, belonged to a wealthy and powerful family—the Fontenoys. The last of the family, the Marquis of St. Florent, was accused of being concerned in the Cinq Mars conspiracy, was executed, and his lands seized by the crown. The several mansions fell into decay, and this forest became a great resort for the hunters, when this old place was finally purchased by the present proprietor, who, during the times of the nobility, always had his house full; and they do say he has amassed large sums of money, which he hoards. I often wonder, if he has so much money, why he allowed his only son, at the age of eighteen, to be marched off to the wars. They have never heard of him since. Report says he was no loss to the old couple, for he was a wild, dissolute, bad young man. Dame Durand herself declares they are very poor. I have heard my uncle say the times are changing, and that this inn will again revive, for it stands on a great thoroughfare, and the forest is full of game of all sorts."

Feeling somewhat tired, after their rough day's journey, Mademoiselle de Morni and our heroine retired early to their chamber, and having dismissed their attendants, were very soon in a tranquil sleep. It was not, however, till a late hour of the night that all the various persons, in the huge building, were buried in repose. How long our heroine slept she could not say, but she was suddenly

awoke by a noise. She started up, but was
amazed by the bright light that illumined the
room; she rubbed her eyes to be satisfied it
was no illusion; but the light was still strong
and at times intense, and a strange noise rung
in her ears. Alarmed, she shook Eugenie,
who woke up with a start.

"Good God!" exclaimed Annie, springing
out of bed, " the house is on fire."

" Pull the bell, pull the bell," exclaimed
mademoiselle, springing out of bed, and rushing
to the front window; but the strong glare
of fire came through a large aperture looking
into the corridor, across which was a crimson
curtain. Presently, as the two girls rapidly
dressed themselves, various bells rung, and
then were heard wild shouts and screams. By
this time the girls had dressed themselves,
though trembling with agitation, and ran to
unlock their door. A tramp of many feet was
heard, the door was burst open, and a dense
volume of flames and smoke burst in, smother-
ing and overpowering them, so that they

staggered back and fell insensible on the bed.
When Eugenie recovered recollection she
looked wildly about her. Her own attendants, half-dressed and slightly scorched, were
crowding about her in a state of distraction.
They were in one of the chambers of the
west wing.

"Where is Mademoiselle Mortimer?" said
Eugenie, starting up in fearful agitation.
"Since I was rescued, so must she be, for we
fell together on the bed. Go and see where
she is."

The entire vicinity was roused. Upwards
of fifty men were using every means to sub-
due the fire, which appeared to have commenced in one of the chambers in the
corridor, where Mademoiselle de Morni and
our heroine slept. A scene of terrible confusion ensued. Monsieur Durand, a man of
some twenty years, was like a maniac. He
was tearing the hair from his head, hurling
maledictions upon all about him, accusing
everyone of breaking open his chest, and

robbing him of the savings of years; whilst Eugenie, in a state of fearful excitement, was seeking everyone, and making distracted enquiries for her friend; but no one had seen Mademoiselle Mortimer. There was an abundance of water, so that in four hours the fire was totally extinguished, after destroying only the corridor, and two or three chambers in the gallery and the back stairs, and the landlord's private store room.

Eugenie, fainting with exertion and distraction, lay exhausted on a sofa in one of the chambers of the east wing. In vain, with tears, she implored those around her to institute a more vigorous search; but, incomprehensible as it appeared, no one recollected seeing Miss Mortimer.

The persons who broke into the chamber, where she and her friend slept, were mostly her own male domestics and the people of the house. Stephen Morlaix, Monsieur de Hauteville's principal attendant, declared that, blinded by the smoke that filled the room, he staggered forward against the bed, and grasping a female form he with great difficulty got out of the room, blinded and half suffocated, and then, rushing through another chamber, got down the front stairs. The rest of the men, who had followed Stephen Morlaix into the room, declared they became bewildered and blinded, and with difficulty got out, thinking the ladies had been rescued, as they could find no one in the chamber. The room was mostly consumed, so far as the bed and all the furniture went. Still, it was very evident no one had been burnt in it.

A strict search was made all over the house, in fact within and without; but no trace of Miss Mortimer could be found; her extraordinary disappearance mystified everyone.

Old Durand was raving and out of his senses; he repeatedly exclaimed, in his fits of delirium, that he saw his son enter his room, smash in the head of his great chest and take his money; he declared he took ten thousand francs in gold. He also affirmed it was his son who had fired the house to rob him. These declarations were regarded as the effects of madness. No one believed he had such a sum, and as to his son, no one had heard anything about him for the last five years. Dame Durand asserted, though in a terrified state herself, that her husband must be insane; they had no such sum of money, and their son was with the army.

The old man certainly slept in a room by himself, and after a time the fire was traced, and seemed to have begun close to his chamber, if not in it. He was insensible when extricated, but most probably more from the smoke than any injury. There were traces also on the window of the room leading to that in which Mademoiselle de Morni and our heroine slept of remnants of damp hay partly consumed.

Monsieur de Hauteville's confidential attendant, after the strictest investigation, was of opinion that the fire was the work of incendiaries and not accidental. He carefully examined everyone that slept that night in the house, but he could not discover if any stranger had been seen by any member of the household during the time of the fire or before or after it.

Eugenie de Morni was bewildered, though relieved to a certain extent by the knowledge that her beloved friend, for she did love her truly and well, had not perished by the fire. She still hoped, strange and mysterious as was her disappearance, that she would be found. One of the domestics was at once despatched on horseback to meet Monsieur de Hauteville, and hasten his arrival, for Eugenie greatly trusted to his sagacity and forethought to solve this strange mystery.

Dame Morelle the old house-keeper of the chateau, who always visited Auray when the family changed residences, took our heroine's disappearance greatly to heart, for she had become much attached to the fair English girl.

About three o'clock in the day De Hauteville

gallopped into the court-yard of the Bois
Rouge greatly agitated; he had met the
messenger five leagues from the auberge, and
being splendidly mounted, had urged his
horse to its greatest speed. When within two
leagues of the auberge, in passing through
the forest of St. Florent, he had had a narrow
escape of his life,—the great pace he was
going at the time no doubt saved his life—
two muskets had been levelled at him from
behind a thick cover. One ball cut his stirrup
leather in two, inflicting a slight wound in
the horse's side; the other whistled past close
to his head.

His first impulse was to check his steed,
drawing a pistol from his pistol holster, but
second thoughts shewed him the impossibility
of a pursuit of an enemy through a thick
wood on horseback, and alone. So again
giving reins to his horse, he continued his
speed till he drew bridle in the court-yard
of the Bois Rouge.

Stephen Morlaix uttered an exclamation of

anger and surprise when he saw the bleeding side of his master's horse and the cut stirrup leather.

"Never mind this trifle now, Morlaix," said De Hauteville, "tell one of your men to mount a fleet horse, and be ready to start in ten minutes for Masle. I must have a score of the Chasseurs-à-Cheval here as soon as possible. I will write a line to their captain."

He then turned into the saloon where Mademoiselle de Morni sat overwhelmed in grief, and where the old housekeeper was applying a lotion to her arm, which was scorched.

"Mon Dieu, my dear Eugenie," exclaimed De Hauteville, "you are hurt; the messenger said nothing of this."

"It is nothing, uncle, a mere scorch, as you may see."

"Yes, yes, I see but, nevertheless, you must have passed through flame. I am distracted at this most mysterious outrage,—but give me pen and ink, I must have a party of chasseurs here at once to scour the country; some villains attempted my life as I rode through St. Florent."

" Mon Dieu!" exclaimed Eugenie, amazed, "attempted your life,—robbers, in broad daylight."

" No, no," muttered De Hauteville, writing rapidly. " Not robbers."

Having having writing, he summoned Stephen Morlaix, gave him the letter, and desired him to tell the messenger to ride hard, and let nothing stop him till he had delivered the paper to Captain Muskien. Then, leaning back in his chair, he said calmly,

" Now, Eugenie, tell me everything that has occurred to you since you left the chateau ?'

" Nothing occurred, Louis, on the road, except our getting into a deep rut, and breaking our traces."

" Did you meet or see at a distance any party of men, or anything unusual."

" No, we passed, of course, now and then some peasants and some carts. When we stuck in the hole, a person on horseback with another man, also mounted, accosted us, and politely asked us if they could assist us. I said no, and they rode on."

" Did you ever see this person before—how was he dressed?"

" He was attired in a military undress, shabby enough. I never saw him before. But I recollect, Annie started when she heard his voice, though she said he was an utter stranger to her."

De Hauteville remained buried in thought several moments; then again calling Stephen Morlaix, went out with him and commenced a strict investigation of that part of the auberge where the fire had taken place. He summoned every soul that had slept in the house that night, and separately examined them. He then visited the landlord, who was extremely ill, and certainly not exactly in his senses. After four hours' investigation of the inmates of the auberge, and of every room in the mansion, he returned to the saloon his niece occupied, and threw himself, jaded and much agitated, into a chair, desiring an attendant to bring some of the wine sent on in hampers.

Having drank a few glasses, he seemed a little roused from his despondency.

" Well, my dear uncle," said Eugenie, anxiously, " have you come upon any clue to unravel this mysterious affair ?"

" Mysterious it is, niece," said De Hauteville, " and, as yet, I have only satisfied myself on one point."

" What is that, uncle ?"

" Why, that Paul Durand, our landlord, has been robbed, and that there is even a probability that his son is the robber."

" Mais, mon Dieu ! Is that possible ! What, rob his own father ! And what could he have to do with our poor Annie ? Besides, the old man had a narrow escape of being burned to death."

" Very likely ; and if it was his son, who, I understand, is a most depraved young villain, and has often threatened his father's life, his intention was to burn or destroy his father."

"Horrible, horrible," said Eugenie, shuddering; "but had the old man really anything to lose?"

"Yes, yes," returned De Hauteville. "Dame Durand confessed to me, he had several thousand francs in a strong chest under his bed; he is a miser, and has hoarded money for years. He never allowed any one to enter his sleeping chamber, which he has always locked and kept the key himself; he always retired to rest early, and locked himself in. Now, the lock of his door is not broken, neither was the door forced, though burned nearly through; his chest is smashed and cleared out, and though he raves wildly, still he persists that he distinctly saw his son. I tried to get from him how his son was dressed, but he rambled away to his gold. By-the-by, what do you suppose was the age of the traveller who spoke to you on the road, and what was he like?"

" He was a tall man, but so bearded that you could only distinguish his eyes: they were black, fierce eyes; his age, I should say, four or five and thirty."

" Paul Durand is not six and twenty, and has fair hair, and blue eyes. There was another man with this stranger, did you get a look at him?"

" I did not bestow much notice on him; he appeared a kind of domestic, but I know his beard and moustache were dark. Still, uncle, allowing either of those strangers to be Paul Durand, what could he possibly gain by carrying off Annie?"

" Ah, there's the mystery," said De Hauteville, jumping up and pacing the chamber, greatly agitated.

Several mounted domestics returned at dark, having scoured the country round for miles without meeting a single human being on whom the slightest suspicion could be fixed. Late that night the troop of chasseurs, arrived, and early the next morning Monsieur de Hauteville, also mounted and armed, left the auberge, leaving the distressed Mademoiselle de Morni to await his return.

CHAPTER V.

We left our hero on board the Belle Poule, making the best of his way to the port of Lisbon. The despatches he carried were important, and he was urged, if possible, to reach his destination before the fleet of Sir John Jervis should have put to sea. To accomplish this object he carried all sail day and night, but the wind, though fresh, was scant. A most careful watch was kept, for it was very natural to expect to meet French cruisers out of the Vannes, or the mouth of the Loire. The strong breezes, half gales, from the nor'-west kept him within sight of the French coast.

Elated as our hero naturally felt at his

success, and full of hope and sanguine antici-
pation for the future in winning fame and a name
any woman might be proud to bear, there were
moments, and those constantly recurring, when
he thought of Annie, a prisoner in the power
of a man whose conduct, to regard it most
favourably, was equivocal. To leave her as
he did was the only way he could hope to release her, but he grieved at the state in which
he had left her, and longed to reach England that he might make an effort to restore
her to liberty and happiness.

One morning, about two hours after sunrise,
just as the young commander made out that
the Belle Poule was off Isle Dieu and the
Island of Noirmoutiers, he perceived, standing
out across his course from the island, a ship,
under top-sails and top-gallant sails; this
vessel, he felt satisfied, was a French cruiser,
and very shortly afterwards discovered her to
be a corvette, with the tri-colour flying at her
peak.

" As we are standing now," said our hero,

to the midshipman, McDonald, " that corvette
will most probably cross our bows. She carries, no doubt, sixteen or eighteen twelve-
pounders, and, I dare say, three times our
complement of men. As we are sailing with
despatches, it will not do to run risks ; if we
can outsail her it will be all right."

" But she will pass too close, sir. She will
recognise us as an enemy."

" I do not know that," said our hero ;
"just send all the men below, except three or
four, keep below yourself, and send Tom
Darking aft."

Tom came aft, rubbing his hands, and eye-
ing the advancing corvette with a grim smile.

" It will not do, Tom," said Lieut. Chamberlain. " It's out of the question, for I see
you are thinking I shall show fight; but not
this time. Just take half-a-dozen of the men,
and get them to put on the French pilot coats
and jackets ; we have a store of them. And
get out the Belle Poule's privateer flag and
number."

All this was done before the French corvette had reached within shot; and also, for fear the ruse should fail, and the corvette prove the fastest under sail, the guns were shotted, and the eighteen-pound carronade cleared for action. There was not a man on board the Belle Poule, that did not inwardly hope that an action would ensue, they felt so confident of their young commander's skill, courage, and good fortune.

Our hero went below, but soon returned upon deck, attired in one of the late Captain Malin's coats and hat, and coolly waited till the corvette should cross them within hail, not altering his course a single point.

The corvette was a remarkably fine-looking craft, but somehow she did not strike our hero as a very fast sailer. He could perceive a number of men on the deck. Instead of passing across the Belle Poule's bows, the corvette paid off, and running past the schooner's stern, luffed up, and, bracing her yards and hauling in tacks and sheets, she

came upon the same tack, and instantly
hailed, saying, "Is the schooner the Belle
Poule?"

"Oui, monsieur," answered our hero, through
a speaking-trumpet.

"Where from?" demanded an officer, also
through a trumpet, for they were some distance asunder, our hero purposely keeping
closer to the wind, having previously gradually
kept away.

"From Brest," answered Lieut. Chamberlain.

"Are there any English vessels of war off
Brest?" demanded the Frenchman.

"Oui, monsieur; four ships of war and a
large frigate, — part of Lord Bridport's
squadron."

"Where are you bound to now?" demanded the lieutenant of the corvette.

"Bourdeaux," said our hero. "What's the
name of the corvette?"

"The Berceau, Captain André Coudin."

The corvette then braced round her topsails

and fell astern of the Belle Poule, who immediately braced her yards sharp on a wind,
and resumed her course. The corvette, after
standing in for the land for some eight or ten
minutes, suddenly went in stays and stood
after the Belle Poule, firing a gun, and hoist-
ing signals on her mast-head.

The two vessels were then about a musket
shot distant from each other.

"By Jove!" said the young midshipman,
laughing, "the captain suspects us."

"He has found it out too late, then," returned our hero, "for I think with this breeze,
we are more than a match for him. Ah! there
goes another gun." This time the shot cut
away the back stay and some running rigging.
Another and another gun followed, one round
shot knocking the top rail into splinters.

"Run up our colours," said our hero to
Barker, "and stand by, my lads. We will
let him see what we can do. Clear away the
carronade."

The two vessels were in a parallel line; consequently the Belle Poule had to brail her foresail and keep away to deliver her shot. This shot, as they a long time afterwards heard, was one of those eccentric shots as to its execution, that appear, when recorded, almost a myth.

The eighteen-pound ball, aim having been taken by Lieut. Chamberlain himself, entered the corvette's bow port, and after smashing the jib boom to pieces, knocked the end of the windlass into splinters, wounding three men severely, dashed into the cook's sanctum, who was then preparing dinner, knocked his coppers to pieces, tumbling him and his assistant into the lee scuppers, fortunately more frightened than hurt, and then, knocking the skylight over the cabin to atoms, came right into the cabin, smashing the table and all on it, and upsetting the captain and first lieutenant, who were at the moment looking over a large chart. The cause of all this disturbance was

afterwards found snugly laid up in a locker
full of champagne, which, of course, it de-
molished.

There was no second shot required, fo⁻,
deprived of her jib boom, the corvette had to
reduce her after sail till she ran out another
spar, and before that was done, it became
very evident that the Belle Poule was by far
the fastest of the two vessels. A shift of
wind into the north-east during the night,
and increasing into a half gale before morning, sent the Belle Poule rapidly to her
destination. The second day they made the
mouth of the Tagus, a tremendous sea running upon that dangerous bar—so heavy was
the sea, though the gale was only a moderate
one, that no pilot would shew out, so our
hero, knowing his draught of water to be
small, ran the bar, the sea sweeping his deck
fore and aft.

Nevertheless, to the admiration of the
pilots within the bar, the Belle Poule dashed
gallantly through, without damage, passed

between the two forts, and then up the river. One of the pilot boats having come alongside, he learned that the English ships were still at anchor off the Fort of Belem.

This was the second time our hero had visited Lisbon; once before in the Leander. So, running up the ten miles which intervened between the mouth and Fort Belem, he came in sight of the eleven line-of-battle ships then under the orders of Sir John Jervis.

Anchoring according to his pilot's directions, and having attracted the attention of several of the ships of war, as he ran past, Augustus descended into his cabin, telling young McDonald to have the gig ready to take him on board the admiral's ship. A custom-house boat instantly came alongside, but having ascertained the character of the schooner, soon left.

Having made the best toilet he could, his means being extremely limited as to garments, our hero came upon deck, with his despatches in his coat pocket. He then took a look at the ships. The nearest to him was a vessel he instantly recognised as the Culloden, commanded by Captain Thomas Trowbridge. This ship was one of the squadron that had formed the expedition against Santa Cruz,* and our hero was, personally known to the gallant Captain Trowbridge, under whose orders he had served as a lieutenant in the storming of Santa Cruz. He then perceived the Victory, the ship that carried the admiral's flag, so jumping into his gig, he pulled up alongside this famous ship of one hundred guns. As he ascended to the deck he stated to a lieutenant, who had observed his approach, and from whence he came, that he had brought despatches for Sir John Jervis from Lord Bridport, whom he had left off Brest.

The second lieutenant of the Victory looked at our hero from head to foot. Faded and worn as his uniform was, it proved him

---

* We beg to apologise to our readers for one liberty we have taken, and that is making the attack against Santa Cruz to take place before the action off Cape St. Vincent.

to be a naval officer, though only of the rank
of a midshipman; but the fine athletic figure
and handsome features of the wearer, and his
manner, commanded respect and civility. The
lieutenant, nevertheless, said, coldly, " Your
name, sir, if you please; and pray what is the
character of the schooner you just this moment
came from ? "

Before our hero could answer, though there
was a flush on his cheek, an officer in the
uniform of a captain pushed his way through
a group of superior officers who stood near
the gangway, and, laying his hand upon our
hero's shoulder, said, aloud, " By Jupiter, the
dead is come to life, or you are the ghost
of Mr. Chamberlain.   Let me feel your fin,
my lad," and the gallant Trowbridge held
out his hand.   " I am rejoiced to be sure you
are no ghost."

" Captain Trowbridge," said our hero, with
a smile of pleasure, as the blunt but gallant
seaman shook him heartily by the hand.

" By Jove, this is surprising," cried Captain

Trowbridge. "We all reckoned you food for sharks, and here you are. I heard you say you had despatches from Lord Bridport. Come along with me, and I will introduce you to Sir John, and then you shall come to the Culloden, and tell me how the deuce you escaped from that most disastrous affair off Santa Cruz. Yonder you see the Captain, seventy-four, Commodore Nelson commands her. He was another of the unfortunates at Santa Cruz, and lost his arm there."

Captain Trowbridge then conducted our hero into the cabin, and, with very little ceremony, introduced him to Sir John, who was dictating a letter to a secretary, as the bearer of an important despatch from Admiral Bridport.

Our hero bowed and handed the admiral the despatch, which led to the famous action off Cape St. Vincent. Leaving Sir John to read his letters, Captain Trowbridge took our hero upon deck, and after introducing him to the first lieutenant of the Victory as a gallant young friend of his, left him to return to the cabin, anxious to hear what Lord Bridport had communicated to the admiral.

" How many ships, Mr. Chamberlain, were there off Brest when you left?" questioned the lieutenant of the Victory.

" Four line-of-battle ships, sir, and the Indefatigable."

" Is not that schooner you came here in a French craft ?   She certainly is not British."

" Yes," said our hero; " she was a French privateer, called the Belle Poule."

" Ah! I thought she was French," returned the lieutenant.   " Who captured her ? she struck me as a remarkably fast sailor as you ran up.   I happened to have my glass upon you."

" By a remarkable chance," said our hero, " I gained possession of her, after a rather tough contest."

The lieutenant seemed surprised; but Captain Trowbridge returning on deck, came up to our hero, saying, " You have brought us very important news. We shall be under weigh all of us before twenty-four hours are over. There is a private letter from Sir Edward Pellew, in which he speaks of you very highly indeed; tells us that you made a very gallant capture not only of the privateer Belle Poule, but also of a fine cutter, the Sans Pareil, and with most desperate odds against you. Sir John knew your father well, and he said the son is walking in the steps of the father. He will see you to-morrow. In the meantime, come with me to my ship; by Jove, I must have some account of how the deuce you got away from Santa Cruz."

Taking leave of the first lieutenant of the Victory, who looked surprised, Captain Trowbridge entered his own gig with our hero, and in a few minutes they were standing on the deck of the Culloden, seventy-four. After an excellent dinner, to which several officers of the Culloden were invited, two or three of whom our hero recognized, and knew him also to be a great favourite

and protégé of Captain Boulder, Thompso,n
of the Leander, a very pleasant evening was
spent, and all listened with great surprise to
a very brief and modest narrative of his
adventures from the time of his leaving Santa
Cruz.

In his narrative our hero carefully avoided
mentioning the family of the Mortimers,
upon whom his thoughts were constantly
fixed.   But for his anxiety to return to
England, and learn what steps had been
taken by Mr. Calthurst, he would have felt
highly elated and pleased with his situation.
Patronised by Captain Trowbridge, and noticed by Sir John Jervis—he was fêted and
made much of by the officers of the several
ships.   He took care to procure a good sup-
ply of garments and uniforms at Lisbon.

Sir John Jervis on the third day had
hoisted the signal to all the captains of the
several ships to get ready for sea, and to
weigh anchor on the fourth.   Previous to this
our hero had been honoured by an interview

with Sir John Jervis, who received him graciously, spoke very kindly of his father as an old and esteemed comrade, and hinted he had heard that his own conduct was much approved.

" For the present," said Sir John, " I wish to take your schooner into the service. You may—as I am told your vessel is exceedingly fast—be of considerable use to me, and you shall not lose by the service. You will be provisioned, and supplied with whatever you may require, and if you are short of hands you can have a dozen."

Our hero thanked Sir John for his kindness, and trusted that circumstances might occur to render his services useful.

" You may consider your time as lieutenant goes on from the period Lord Bridport appointed you to your present command."

At the stated time the eleven ships lying in the Tagus got under weigh, and stood for the mouth of the river. On board the Belle Poule all were in high spirits—they had all entered their names as able seamen, ready to serve his Majesty on the deck of whatever ship they might be required. The elder Barker, an excellent seaman, was appointed first mate, Tom Darking second, and as to Master Donald McDonald, he admired his situation amazingly. He declared that his skipper was a generous and fine fellow, kind and careful of his men; provisioned his vessel better than any vessel in the fleet, from his private purse. Having drawn a bill upon his agent in London, he had plenty of cash, and he spent it like a gentleman. There were two-and-thirty fine able-bodied men on board the Belle Poule, which having been re-painted and almost re-rigged, excited universal admiration ; her graceful hull and taper masts having quite a yacht-like appearance.

It was not the good fortune of Sir John Jervis to get his small fleet out of the Tagus without mishap. The ninety-eight-gun ship, St. George, unfortunately ran foul of a Portuguese frigate, and afterwards went aground upon the South Cachop, striking very heavily, and unshipping her rudder. The Belle Poule seeing the disaster, and having so little draught of water, immediately ran alongside. The crew of the St. George were then cutting away her fore and mizen-masts to ease her. The officers of the St. George felt this disaster exceedingly. A powerful cable was got on board the Belle Poule, and an anchor; this was carried out to some distance to windward, and then a strain was put upon it, to heave her off. The St. Albans then came to her assistance, and finally she was got off, but was obliged to return to Lisbon, to repair. The rest of the vessels proceeded to the rendezvous off Cape St. Vincent, where they were joined by five sail of the line and one frigate, as promised in Lord Bridport's despatches.

Whilst the fleet remained off the Cape, hoping to hear of, or fall in with the great Spanish squadron, our hero, in his schooner, was sent on towards Cadiz, to have a look-out

for the ships Sir John was so anxious to fall in
with.

Working-up against a strong south-easterly
breeze, the Belle Poule the second day gained
sight of two large Spanish line-of-battle ships
standing in for Cadiz. The next morning
presented an imposing sight—in fact, the
grand fleet of Spain, under the command
of Don Josef de Cordova, was in full sail,
and, no doubt, bound through the Straits,
intending a junction with the French fleet.

Being satisfied that he had tidings of importance to communicate, our hero bore up;
but was shortly afterwards chased by a Spanish brig. The wind was blowing very strong
from the nor'-east, which was adverse to the
Spanish fleet in their attempt to make Cadiz.
The brig was not a fast sailer, and our
hero, finding he could sail two feet for her
one, and anxious to do something creditable
before he rejoined the fleet, gradually coaxed
this Spanish brig to chase by trailing a huge
sail overboard, waited, till he had enticed

her a considerable distance from any of the
Spanish ships-of-war, and then called his men
aft.

"Now, my lads," he said, " I have no time
for long shots, or short; I want to take that
brig. She's only a Spaniard. Barker will
put you alongside, and in less than twenty
minutes after 1 expect she will be ours. No
cheering, my lads; no noise; but prepare
yourselves, for, mind you, it's two to one or
more."

Tom Darking sent his hat flying in his
ecstasy, and all the crew tightened their belts,
re-primed their pistols, and had a rub at their
cutlasses.

The sail was hauled in, and to the intense
amazement of the dons, who considered the
schooner a slow sailer and an easy prize, she
suddenly bore away, and in five minutes run
her on board with a smart shock, receiving
the discharge of the Spaniard's broadside as a
thing of naught.

Our hero, cutlass in hand, was the first on

the enemy's deck, and the whole crew, young McDonald at their head, followed, with a cheer that electrified the crew. Nevertheless, though there were sixty-five seamen in the brig, and the officers fought well, the British drove all before them, and our hero, singling out the captain, disarmed him, after a contest of two or three minutes.

Tom Darking, cutting his way to the halyards, hauled down the Spanish flag, cheering vociferously, whilst the astounded Spaniards threw down their arms and fled below, where they were securely fastened down.

In this short contest there were only two Spaniards killed, and one officer and the skipper wounded. Some of the Belle Poule's men had slight wounds, and our hero received a mere scratch; the midshipman, McDonald, met with no further damage than a good ducking, for, rushing at a tall powerful Spaniard, who had just broken his cutlass, the man seized him in his arms and threw him overboard; but the midshipman was not so easily disposed of, he swam alongside the schooner, and was picked up by the first mate with a boat hook.

"Now, my lads," said our hero, "let us lose no more time; this is a fine brig, but look out, for there's either a small frigate or a corvette bearing down upon us; we have four miles the start of her, and before she overhauls us we shall be in sight of some of our look-out ships."

Taking the captain of the brig and his four officers on board the "Belle Poule," and leaving the first mate, Barker, and twelve hands, well armed in the brig, both vessels crammed on all sail, and stood away for Cape St. Vincent, half buried in the seas with the pressure of canvas they carried.

It was a frigate that chased the Belle Poule and the captured brig. There would have been very little chance for our hero in the thin half-gale of wind that suddenly sprung up; for the Spanish frigate in pursuit was a very smart vessel, had not two British frigates appeared in sight, making to windward just as she came within shot commenced firing her bow guns. The Spaniard no sooner sighted these two frigates, than she shortened sail, hove up in the wind, and at once stood back to join the grand fleet. The two frigates were the Lively and Niger.

Our hero questioned the Spanish captain, who, disgusted and enraged, stood regarding him with looks of rage and mortification.

Captain Don Pablo Loberane spoke French. He complained bitterly, when addressed by our hero, of his mode of attack. He said it was "*Barbarous*—out of all recognised usages. His crew were attacked as if by a band of pirates or wild Indians."

Lieutenant Chamberlain could afford to smile at the Spaniard's rage and reproaches. He begged him to excuse his method of attack ; but said he really had no time for a contest after the Spaniard's approved mode of engaging, as he was anxious to get back to the British ships, who would, no doubt, commence a contest with the Spanish fleet according to his preconceived notions of etiquette. He then civilly requested to know the name of the brig.

"She is called the 'Glorioso,' monsieur. Carries fourteen twelve-pounders, and a crew of officers and men amounting in all to forty-eight men and four boys. What is the name of this schooner? You had a numerous crew for so small a vessel."

"Pardon me, Don Pablo," returned our hero, " our officers and crew amount to thirty-two only."

The Spanish skipper looked at his first lieutenant, his yellow skin turning a pale saffron.

Before night, the Belle Poule and her prize ran in amongst the fleet, creating considerable curiosity on board the Culloden, near which ship she hove to : and ten minutes afterwards our hero was on the deck of the admiral's ship, informing him that the Spanish fleet,

above thirty ships altogether, and amongst
them the celebrated Santissima Trinidada, of
a hundred and thirty guns, was not five
leagues off.

CHAPTER IV.

IT is not our intention to weary our readers with details of the celebrated battle off Cape St. Vincent, in which the British ships, numbering only fifteen, gained a glorious victory over the finest fleet Spain ever sent to sea, and numbering thirty-one ships.

Our hero had the choice of service on the deck of either the Captain, Commodore Nelson, or the Culloden ; his choice was the Culloden, commanded by his kind friend, Captain Trowbridge, but, owing to the Culloden running foul of the Colossus, and getting considerably damaged, he missed her, and got on board the Captain—his schooner

lying to at some distance, and the brig
Glorioso having been sent to Lisbon.

By this change of ship, Augustus Chamberlain had the honour of serving under
England's greatest Admiral, and when the
Captain, towards the close of the engagement,
fell foul of the San Nicholas, he was one of
the few that followed the gallant Nelson
through the upper quarter gallery window of
the San Nicholas, and rendering the Admiral
an essential service, as they fought their way
to the poop, where they found Captain Berry
in possession. Here the Spanish officers delivered up their swords.

Directly after the engagement, our hero
sailed in the Belle Poule for Plymouth, with
a brief despatch for the Admiralty, and a
private letter from Commodore Nelson to one
of the Lords. Thus conveying to England
the news of one of the most important victories
England ever gained at sea, and for which
Sir John Jervis was created Earl St. Vincent,
and all the first lieutenants commanders.

Our hero was extremely short-handed, for ten of his crew, and his first mate, Barker, were gone to Lisbon in the Glorioso brig, which turned out to be a most valuable prize. They were to land their prisoners, and then proceed to Plymouth. Baffling winds and squally weather for two days, retarded the Belle Poule's progress. The third morning the wind veered to the eastward, blowing a gale, and before night, whilst a tremendous storm broke over the Atlantic with unusual violence, our hero had struck both top-masts, lowered the yards on deck, and made everything as snug as possible; under a treble-reefed topsail and a storm stay-sail, the Belle Poule lay to. But the sea became tremendous, making a clean sweep over her deck. With difficulty they saved their two boats, the gig was stove in pieces, and the cook's caboose and all its materials swept over the side. It was a trying time, but the Belle Poule proved herself an incomparable sea-boat. This severe gale and storm, with the weather thick, lasted without intermission for three days, during which the crew suffered severely by being continually wet. The fourth morning the sky suddenly broke to the north, and a gleam of sunshine was shed over the storm-tossed sea; the gale moderated, and the horizon cleared. About ten o'clock in the morning, the sea having become calmer, and the sky still clearing, our hero swept the horizon with his glass. The next moment an object, some six miles to windward, attracted his attention. The sea being still exceedingly high and troubled, he could not at once say what kind of craft he beheld, but after a time he made her out to be a ship without sail, with only her three lower masts standing, and rolling tremendously. Shaking out his reefs, and setting more sail, he commenced tacking up towards the strange ship. Tom Darking was at the wheel, and as our hero kept his eye on the stranger, he said, " Perhaps she's a Frenchman, sir!"

" It's quite possible, Tom. It is a vessel of

war, at all events, for as she rolls over I can see her ports. If French, in her disabled state, she is more at our mercy than we at hers. Half-an-hour will tell."

Young Mc Donald coming on deck, our hero requested him to get the tri colour hoisted. " We shall soon see the stranger's flag, if she has a halyard left to hoist it."

The wind and sea were rapidly settling down, and the sun shining bright and cheeringly. All hands came on deck, anxiously looking towards the stranger. They were soon within a mile, and tacking, stood right for her. Lieutenant Chamberlain, after steadily regarding her, said to Mc.Donald, " She's a French corvette of eighteen guns, and if 1 am not greatly mistaken, it is the same corvette, the Berceau, that chased us from Belle Isle, on our voyage to Lisbon."

Two or three of the old men-of-war's men looked with very greedy eyes upon the cor-vette. Her deck was crowded with men, who were to be seen preparing to hoist a jury-yard and sail to the foremast, and also on the mizen; and as the Belle Poule advanced, up went the revolutionary banner of France, and at the same time two of her bow guns were discharged at the advancing schooner, but, owing to her heavy rolling, the balls went high over the Belle Poule.

"Ah!" exclaimed our hero, " they recognise us. She has lost all her yards and spars in the late gale; but is not otherwise injured."

"Now, my lads," he continued, "we are not going to be shot at without returning the compliment. We cannot take possession of that vesssel, that's certain; but we can make her strike her colours, I think, and by that time some English ship may heave in sight. We must not let them set any sail. We can work round and round her, and clear her crowded decks with our carronade. So now, let us to our work; but get our yards up, and our topsail set the first thing."

Keeping out of shot of the corvette, which

kept drifting to leeward, several of her crew being employed rigging haulyards and to hoist their yard and foresail; but before they were near ready the Belle Poule had set her topsail, loaded her long gun with grape and canister, and took up a position within pistol shot of the corvette's bows, after receiving a most harmless broadside from the enraged Frenchman, whose ship was, of course, perfectly unmanageable. Our hero felt loath to fire into the Frenchman, for her crowded decks offered good mark for his long gun. He, therefore, dropped within distance, and taking the trumpet, hailed the corvette, and requested to have their flag hauled down, in order to save a useless waste of life. He was answered by a shout of derision, and a smart discharge of musketry, which fortunately only wounded one man slightly, and knocked off our hero's hat.

The next instant bang went the eighteen-pound carronade, sweeping the deck of the enemy like a shower of iron hail. This fatal discharge rendered the captain of the corvette furious—his second lieutenant and five men were killed, and several wounded; and the schooner being handled like a yacht, he found it utterly impossible to hoist his foresail, or bring his broadside to bear upon his puny but dangerous antagonist.

Two or three more shots from the Belle Poule drove the crew of the corvette below for shelter. But haul down their flag the captain would not; and though he made the men go below, he kept his station with his officers on the quarter-deck.

Our hero then loaded his guns with round shot, and before an hour had elapsed, the corvette had her foremast and mizen so badly damaged that, in a heavy roll, her two masts went over the side.

The captain still kept the deck, and when the colours were shot away, and nothing remained but the mainmast, the commander of the Belle Poule again demanded a surrender.

The French captain, stamping upon the deck, cried out, " Now come, sacre pirate as you are, and take the vessel, if you can."

This our hero knew he could not do, for there were at least a hundred and fifty men on board. Not wishing to kill the commander of the corvette, who was an undoubtedly brave man, our hero ceased firing. Just then one of his men sang out, " A large ship standing owards us, under a press of canvas."

Lieutenant Chamberlain turned his attention upon the stranger. She was a large brig, and was carrying top-gallant sails. When the Belle Poule ceased firing the crew of the corvette came upon deck, watching for an opportunity to sink their impudent antagonist, if he would only give them an opportunity; but the commander had no such intention. They fired their bow guns now and then; but so very unsteady was the corvette that no damage was done to the schooner, beyond cutting away a backstay or a stray rope.

" By Jove!" suddenly exclaimed our hero, " That is our prize, the Glorioso."

Three tremendous cheers were given by the crew of the Belle Poule, which greatly discomfited the crew of the corvette. The brig had recognised the schooner, and she immediately ran up signals to that effect, and then the Belle Poule stood towards her, and on the brig's coming up, they hove to within hail.

Our hero learned that they had left Lisbon, after landing their prisoners, and were ordered to Plymouth. They had left Lisbon four days before our hero quitted the fleet, and had escaped the great fury of the tempest, only coming in for the tail-end of it.

Our hero told his first mate his adventure with the French corvette, and his determination, now he was come up, to capture her; but as it was impossible to board her, the only way was to take her in tow.

" But," said Jem Barker, " they will cut away the tow-ropes."

" I have thought of that," returned Lieutenant Chamberlain, " but I have several very heavy chains. The water is smooth enough for our purpose—so put out your long boat, with four hands, and come alongside."

In the meantime the crew of the corvette were working with might and main to hoist a sail on the mainmast, so as to get their ship before the wind; but the Belle Poule was not going to let them do that so easily.

As soon as the brig's boat came alongside Tom Darking with four hands, all that could be spared, jumped in. Two heavy and powerful chains were put into the boat; these chains had belonged to the St. George, and were put into the Belle Poule, at the time she ran aground, to assist in getting her off, and were forgotten to be returned. These chains were to be passed through the hawse holes of the corvette, and to them strong cables were to be attached, and thus the brig and schooner would take the corvette in tow.

To protect the crew of the boat during this somewhat perilous exploit, the schooner

took up her position across the bows of
the corvette, and drove the exasperated
Frenchmen from their two bow guns, killing
several and wounding twice as many, whilst
a splinter, as they afterwards learned, struck
the captain, knocking him down stunned upon
the deck.

Our hero, who beheld this accident, ordered
the firing to cease, permitting some of
his men to remove the captain below.

Under the protection of this destructive
carronade, the boat's crew performed their
task without the loss of a man, though twice
the Frenchmen made a rush to cast off the
chains, but the carronade swept the deck, and
a cross fire from the brig drove the maddened
Frenchmen below.

After the chains were passed and united,
cables were attached, and before an hour had
expired the schooner and brig had the
corvette in tow. Still the crew of the French
ship made desperate efforts to free themselves
and work their guns.

The Bellé Poule and the brig suffered considerable damage in sails and rigging, but the brig hauled two of her twelve-poun lers aft; these and the carronade so swept the corvette's decks, shattering her bulwarks, and tearing up her deck, that at length the officers and crew gave up in despair, and sullenly retired below.

It was a work of considerable difficulty, owing to the corvette not having the command of her rudder; but the next morning a British man-of-war, the Petrel, came up with them, and, on hailing the Belle Poule, was informed that the corvette was a prize. This created considerable surprise.

An officer belonging to the corvette hailed and offered to surrender. His captain was, he said, badly hurt, and more than thirty men more or less wounded, besides eleven killed.

Our hero boarded his prize, with a few men, and in a very short time managed to run up a spare topsail on the main-mast

and put two of his men at the wheel. She
then steered easily. The Petrel kept their
company till within sight of the Start light-
house, and then, giving them a hearty parting
cheer, bore away for Lisbon.

Before night the Belle Poule, the brig, and
their prize, were safely at anchor in the
Plymouth Sound. As it was necessary that
our hero should instantly proceed with his
despatches to London, he at once waited
upon the proper authorities in Plymouth and
handed over his prizes, and communicated
the news of the famous battle off Cape St. Vincent and the dispersing, capture, and destruction of the great Spanish squadron by Admiral
Sir John Jervis's fleet. The news flew through
Plymouth like wildfire; and as our hero left
for London, posting with four horses, the
loud booming of guns, the peals of bells, and
the shouts and cheers of the mob that followed
his chaise told how important was the intelligence he had communicated.

He travelled all night, and about nine

o'clock the next morning alighted in the
court yard of the White Horse. Having
made a hasty breakfast and a hasty toilet,
he set out for Lord Linwood's mansion in
Grosvenor Square.

The first lord of the Admiralty was an
active man of business, and when our hero
sent in his name stating that he brought
despatches from Sir John Jervis, he was instantly ushered into his presence. His lordship
was taking his breakfast, but the intelligence
that an officer from Sir John Jervis's fleet
wished to deliver an important despatch
banished his appetite for a time.

Lord Linwood looked at our hero with a
keen, searching, inquiring glance, and the
inspection seemed to please him, for he
graciously said, holding out his hand for the
letter, " I hope you are the bearer of good
news—a battle, I suppose."

" Yes, my lord, and I rejoice to tell you
also a glorious victory."

Lord Linwood seized the despatch, tore open the letter, and eagerly read the contents.

"Come, this is very important and most satisfactory intelligence," he said, as he laid down the despatch, and requested our hero to ring the bell. This order was complied with. His lordship then opened Lord Nelson's letter. After reading it, he took another look at our hero, and said, " Let me see you about this time next Thursday, Mr. Chamberlain. You may now retire. My friend Nelson speaks well, indeed, highly of your gallantry. It is a great pity you are so young ; however, that cannot be helped, you will grow older," and again taking up the letters, Admiral Linwood resumed reading, and our hero bowed, and retired.

As he was descending the stairs, and crossing the hall, a door opened, and a young and beautiful girl put forth her head. She looked earnestly at our hero, who bowed. She was pale, and seemed agitated ; but as he was passing on, she came forth and said, her voice almost trembling, " Pray, sir, would you be so kind as to answer me a question or two ? "

" Certainly."

She then slipped back, requesting him to follow her—and when within the room she closed the door, and, to his increased surprise, he found himself alone with the lady. As we said, she was very pale, and considerably agitated.

" I hope you will excuse me," she said hastily, " for the liberty I am taking. You come from Sir John Jervis's fleet, and I—" she hesitated, and then added, " I understand that there has been a great naval battle ? "

" How did she know that ? " thought our hero ; but he at once answered, " Yes, there has been a battle, ending in a glorious victory."

" Ah ! it is a victory, then," she said, somewhat sadly ; " what ship were you in ? "

" During the engagement I served under Commodore Nelson."

The before pale face became crimson, and the delicate white fingers were entwined nervously, as she eagerly asked, "Then you must have known Lieutenant the Honourable St. George Forester?"

"Yes," returned our hero, beginning to guess the object of these enquiries; "yes, and a most gallant officer he is; this brilliant victory will, no doubt, make him a commander."

To our hero's intense surprise, the girl dropped into a seat, exclaiming, "Ah! then I am lost," and covered her face with her hands.

Before, however, our hero could utter another word, the door opened, and a stately-looking lady, richly attired, entered the room.

The girl started up, and removing her hands from her face, our hero could perceive the unmistakeable traces of tears. The lady looked from one to the other with great surprise, and then fixing her keen grey eyes upon our hero, she said stiffly,

" Well, sir, what may be your purpose in this room?"

Before our hero could reply, the girl stepped forward, and, with considerable firmness, said, " I requested this gentleman to enter here," and then turning to our hero she said, looking gratefully into his face, " I thank you, sir, for obliging me, and now I will wish you good morning." Our hero bowed, and taking up his hat left the room, and then the house.

" By Jove! this is rather curious," he muttered to himself, as he walked thoughtfully along the street, " I cannot understand it."

Returning to his hotel, he made some enquiries respecting Mr. Calthurst, and ascertained that the worthy solicitor lived in Welbeck Street, whither he at once proceeded, and finding the residence, enquired of one of the clerks if he could see Mr. Calthurst. He was told that the solicitor was engaged at the Court of Common Pleas on a most important case. The clerk, who seemed

to regard our hero in his undress naval uniform with a great deal of interest, said—

" Who shall I say called, sir?"

" Chamberlain, Lieutenant Chamberlain."

" Bless me, sir!" exclaimed the clerk,
springing from his seat. " Are you the naval
officer who was wrecked with a young lady,
a Miss Mortimer, who most unfortunately
died?"

" Died!" exclaimed our hero, in a voice
of intense excitement, whilst his face flushed.
" Who says Miss Mortimer died? I know to
the contrary, for I saw her alive two months
ago."

" Did you, sir," returned the clerk, quite
excited, " then you had better go at once to
the Court, for Mr. Calthurst is called upon,
for the last time, to show proof that Miss
Mortimer is not dead.. She is stated to have
died four months ago, and the next heir to
her father's property, Sir Herbert Delme,
declares he has proofs of her death."

" He can have no proofs," said our hero,

angrily; "but I will go to the Court this instant," and hastily saluting the clerk, he hurried out of the office.

The young sailor's mind was in great confusion. He felt satisfied that Miss Mortimer was not dead; but would his assertion that he saw her alive two months back be of any avail. Hailing a coach, cabs being yet unthought of, he was driven with all speed to the Court of Common Pleas. Seeing our hero's anxiety and his naval uniform, the driver demanded three times his proper fare, which was paid without hesitation.

" Ah," said coachee, looking with profound regret at his passenger, as he disappeared into the hall, " them's the right sort—them jolly tars. I might as well have axed another bob."

Our hero sent in his card to Mr. Calthurst at the very moment the judge in court was clearly stating the case to the exulting Sir Herbert Delme and his friends

Judge Manning declared that any further

opposition to Sir Herbert Delme's claims to
the entire property of Mr. Mortimer, was
vexatious and uncalled for; the proofs of the
death of Mr. Mortimer, Mrs. Mortimer, and
infant son were indisputable, and also that
Miss Mortimer and a naval officer, of the
name of Chamberlain, who attempted to
save the young lady on a raft, were seen to
perish by the captain of the Cumberland
packet, and several of his crew.   The French
government had also forwarded a document,
signed by a Captain Popatin, the commander
of a strong battery, close to which the bodies
of the two unfortunate young persons were
dashed ashore.

At this moment it was that a clerk of the
court handed our hero's card to Mr. Calthurst.
No sooner did the solicitor read the name,
than he sprang to his feet in intense agitation, his face flushed to the temples.

"Beg your lordship's pardon for inter-
rupting you," exclaimed the solicitor, "but a
most unexpected witness has turned up, and

one whose testimony will, I consider, be quite conclusive, and prove to you that one, at all events, of the unfortunate family of Mr. Mortimer still exists."

" Your witness must produce very strong proofs indeed, Mr. Calthurst," said Sir Herbert Delme's legal adviser, Mr. Gardner, " to upset the evidence before us," and he gazed over at the baronet, who was looking rather startled.

" My witness," returned Mr. Calthurst, calmly, for he had conquered his agitation, " will be able to do so, I have no doubt, and with your permission, my lord, I will introduce him."

" Certainly, certainly," said Judge Manning, " let us see and hear him."

Mr. Calthurst sent one of the clerks, requesting our hero to come into court. A dead silence prevailed, and considerable curiosity and excitement prevailed in the minds of all present, for the subject of dispute was half-a-million of money. Sir Herbert Delme

looked anxious and startled, his friends uneasy, and Mr. Gardner by no means
tranquil.

When Lieutenant Chamberlain entered the
court, and was requested to enter the witness
box, all eyes were turned upon him; his fine
countenance, and graceful figure, seen to advantage in his undress uniform, created a
great sensation, and a strong prepossession in
his favour. Having been sworn, Mr. Gardner, putting on a very important look said,—

" Your name, sir, and profession ?"

" Augustus Chamberlain, lieutenant in the
royal navy !"

Had a bomb-shell exploded in the court,
it could not have created greater sensation.
Sir Herbert Delme turned deadly pale, at
the same time regarding our hero with a look
of undisguised hate.

Mr. Gardner appeared petrified. Judge
Manning alone remained calm and unnerved,
whilst murmurs and smothered exclamations
resounded amongst the audience.

Mr. Gardner coughed, took out his handkerchief, passed it across his face, and then
said, " This is very extraordinary ; you say,
sir," addressing our hero, "that you are
Lieutenant Chamberlain, the same Lieutenant
Chamberlain reported to have perished in
attempting to gain the shore from a raft,
after the wreck of the French gun ship—
the Droits de l' Homme."

" You are quite correct, sir," returned our
hero, " I am ; and on the same raft was Miss
Annie Mortimer, six seamen—two brothers
named Barker,and another man named Thomas
Darking. These three seamen are now in
Plymouth, and can vouch for the truth of
what I tell you, as also for my identity ; the
three others remain prisoners in France."

" How is this ?" said Mr. Gardner, almost
trembling with agitation, " the captain of the
Cumberland packet, in whose ship a midshipman named Chamberlain was a passenger,
declares that the said midshipman and Miss

Mortimer were seen to perish before reaching the shore, and a Captain Popatin signs a document, forwarded by the authorities of Brest, stating that both Miss Mortimer and Midshipman Chamberlain were thrown on the beach, dead."

"Captain Popatin," returned our hero, "I am sorry to say, is a most consummate rascal, if he has signed so false a document. As to Captain Inglis, a brave and kind commander, he might very readily have been deceived, looking from the deck of the wrecked vessel. The raft was certainly upset, and turned over on the surf, which ran exceedingly high, but nevertheless, I was so fortunate as to carry Miss Mortimer on shore alive. Captain Popatin was the first person we encountered, with a dozen of his artillery men. The seamen, who swam ashore further down, were taken prisoners by Captain Popatin's men, and marched off to his battery. Miss Mo ti-mer and myself were hospitably received into·

the chateau of a Monsieur de Hauteville, a general of division, and governor of a very extensive district."

Mr. Gardner looked confounded, whilst Sir Herbert Delme became livid with rage and disappointment. Nevertheless, he said, "This is all very plausible, but we have no proof that you are the Augustus Chamberlain, the midshipman, stated by Captain Inglis and by Captain Popatin to have perished. You may be an—"

"Take care, sir," interrupted our hero, sternly, "what you say. My identity can be easily proved. I yesterday brought despatches from the British fleet to Lord Linwood, and his lordship can vouch for my being Lieutenant Augustus Chamberlain, of His Majesty's ship the Leander."

At the mention of the First Lord of the Admiralty, as a witness to Lieutenant Chamberlain's identity, a profound conviction that all was lost seized upon Sir Herbert Delme's friends and supporters. Mr. Gardner was overpowered—all he could say was,

" Where, Lieutenant Chamberlain, do you say Miss Mortimer is, if she is alive ?"

" I left her in the hospitable mansion of Monsieur de Hauteville, which is within nine miles of Audierne, where the French vessel was wrecked."

" It appears to me, gentlemen," said Judge Manning, " that this case, for the present, must stand over. Mr. Calthurst has now to take steps to restore Miss Mortimer to her country and to freedom. This will end the suit altogether. If Sir Herbert Delme still doubts the existence of Miss Mortimer, he must produce other proofs of her decease than those now before the court, for as to Lieut. Chamberlain's statement, nothing can be clearer or more convincing. It is, of course, possible, though not probable, that Miss Mortimer may have died since his departure from France, three months ago—for death comes to the young as well as to the aged. Therefore, gentlemen, for the present, we adjourn the court."

CHAPTER VII.

BEFORE leaving the court, Mr. Calthurst had a short conference with Lieut. Chamberlain, begging the favour of his company to dinner.

"We can then," said the solicitor, "fully and clearly converse on a subject I can well imagine most interesting to you, in fact to both of us; for instant steps must be taken to release or ransom Miss Mortimer. At all events, we must have convincing proofs of her existence, for it is now three months since you escaped from France. Depend upon it, Sir Herbert Delme, as heir at law, will leave no stone unturned to secure the immense property of Mr. Mortimer."

Promising to be punctual to the time, our

hero, full of thought, look leave of the solicitor. Between the interval of the dinner, however, we will briefly lay before our readers what had occurred in the Calthurst family after the period of the solicitor's clerk absconding with the will of Mr. Mortimer. No trace of the clerk could be gained, though neither money nor exertions were spared by Mr. Calthurst, whilst a severe domestic calamity gave the vexed solicitor another turn to his thoughts. His youngest daughter had eloped, and at the expiration of a week, he received a most penitent letter from "Lady Delme." Mr. Calthurst felt this blow severely. Bella was his favourite child, and pardon this imprudent step he would not. Neither the mother's entreaties, with the son's and the eldest daughter's added, had the slightest effect. He detested the character of Sir Herbert Delme, and he severely blamed his wife, whom he felt sure had been a party to a disreputable match with a titled spendthrift and reckless adventurer.

Mrs. Calthurst became furious at his reproaches ; she gloried, she declared, in the
grand match her daughter had so cleverly
made with a man of rank and fortune.

" Fortune ! " bitterly repeated Mr. Calthurst. " He's not worth a shilling ; and besides owes above thirty thousand pounds to
Jews."

" What's that," triumphantly retorted Mrs.
Calthurst, " to a man who will inherit half a
million ? "

" He will never inherit a shilling of Mr.
Mortimer's wealth," observed the lawyer,
bitterly. " I will take care of that. It shall
never be said I connived at my daughter's
marriage with a man whom I knew would inherit my client's fortune."

" We shall see," said Mrs. Calthurst, " what
the law will say to that. Sir Herbert has
obtained undoubted evidence of Miss Mortimer's death, and you yourself have acknowledged that you have authentic proofs of the

deaths of Mr. and Mrs. Mortimer and their infant son."

" I will dispute his claims as long as I possess a shilling," retorted the husband. " I will recover the lost will, if it costs me ten thousand pounds. Besides, 1 do not believe that proofs of Miss Mortimer's death have been obtained."

" How can you be so obstinate ?" said Mrs. Calthurst, " and also so blind to the advantages we shall obtain by this marriage of our daughter. What a connection for our son and other daughter. They will be able to mix with the highest of the aristocracy when Sir Herbert gains his just inheritance. Has not Mrs. Cope, Mrs. Mortimer's attached attendant, plainly told you that Miss Mortimer with some young naval officer—Ah ! yes, a midshipman named Chamberlain—embarked on a raft, and that numbers saw them swallowed up by the sea ? My daughter tells me also that Sir Herbert has, at a great expense, got documents over from France, proving the death of this young girl and this midshipman.

" Let us cease this discussion," observed Mr. Calthurst. " I will still have the will, even —which God forbid ! if Miss Mortimer has perished. I will advertise and offer ten thousand pounds for its discovery, and promising no questions will be asked."

" All useless," interrupted the excited Mrs. Calthurst, heedlessly, and not thinking what she uttered, in her excited state. " The will you will never see ; it's destroyed."

Mr. Calthurst was struck down. He sank back, deadly pale, into his chair, exclaiming, in a voice of cutting reproach, " Oh! woman, woman! have *you* been aiding to secure your daughter's misery ?"

Mrs. Calthurst at once saw she had uttered words criminating herself to a certain degree. She trembled and gazed into the almost agonised features of her husband with remorse stamped upon her countenance, for she truly loved him ; but, alas! pride was her beset-

ting sin—pride and love of station. To see
her daughter a lady, she had crushed all
the better feelings of her heart; she became,
in a measure, blind to consequences, and
looked at everything in a different light. By
no means unprincipled, she nevertheless had
gained a knowledge of a great crime, and yet
she regarded that crime as a very venial of-
fence; indeed she argued with herself that it
was most cruel injustice in Mr. Mortimer
to make a will, cutting off his lawful heir, to
leave his wealth to hospitals. Sir Herbert
Delme's vices, which were those of the very
worst kind, she was inclined to consider the
mere effervescence of youth, which a more
mature age and a fond wife would effec-
tually check. Thus, induced by the sophistry
of her son and daughter, assisted by her
darling sin, pride, she secretly aided and
brought about the match between her daughter and Sir Herbert Delme. One thing alone
had checked her, for a moment, in giving her
consent and lending her help to this union,

money was required, as Sir Herbert had
not a shilling. Mrs. Calthurst possessed
some houses in her own right, which her
husband never interfered with. Her son told
her Sir Herbert required about two thousand
pounds to enable him to procure proofs ot
Miss Mortimer's death, and to enable him to
marry Bella, his sister, at once.

Mrs. Calthurst hesitated at first. "There's
one thing makes me a little timid, Bella," said
her mother, in answer to her daughter's and
son's persuasions. "There's that horrid will.
If that is recovered, Mr. Mortimer's wealth
goes to hospitals."

"Be easy, mother, on that head," said the
son, in a whisper; "the will is destroyed, not
a vestige of it exists."

Mrs. Calthurst turned deadly pale; she
could intrigue, but she felt a horror of crime.

"My God! how do you know that, John?"
she exclaimed, in a trembling voice. "Surely
you are not joined with that ungrateful wretch,
Adams?"

" Stuff and nonsense, mother," exclaimed
John Calthurst; "do you take me for a
fool? Listen: that idiot, Adams, contrived
to steal the will. It seems he gambled and
lost a thousand pounds in play. He thought
Sir Herbert Delme would be glad to give him
a couple of thousand or more for the will;
but the baronet indignantly rejected his
offer, and tried to gain possession of the will
to restore it. A violent struggle ensued, and
in a furious rage, Adams threw the will
into the fire, and held Sir Herbert till it
was consumed. 'Now,' said he, 'I will
swear I acted under your directions. You
will not be able to upset my oath. The will
is destroyed, and its destruction gives you
half a million; give me a thousand pounds,
and I quit the country for ever.' What
could Sir Herbert do? No one would believe
his version of the case; so, after some consideration, he consented. If, mother, you
give the baronet two thousand pounds, he
will, with, one thousand, send Thomas Adams

off to America, and marry Bella the day
after, and make her Lady Delme."

Mrs. Calthurst, whether she believed her
son's story or not, considered that her best
plan, as it accorded with her wishes, was to
consent. She therefore raised two thousand
pounds on mortgage, and Bella Calthurst
thus became Lady Delme.

We have said that Mrs. Calthurst was
struck with remorse when she beheld the
grief and dismay depicted on her husband's
features, on hearing her indiscreet assertion
that the will was destroyed. Her first impulse
was to throw herself into his arms and confess her guilty knowledge of the crime committed by Thomas Adams; but her pride
again interfered, and checking the good impulse, she resorted to prevarication, which
widened the breach between them, and broke
up the happiness of a union of twenty-four
years.

Almost broken hearted at the ill-advised
step taken by his daughter, and as he feared,

the mad, unprincipled action of his wife in being a participator in a fearful crime, Mr. Calthurst nevertheless set himself steadily to work to oppose Sir Herbert Delme's claim to the Mortimer property. We have seen the result at the trial at which Judge Manning presided.

Sir Herbert Delme left the court almost in a state of madness; half a million of money had been torn from his grasp, when he considered himself secure in its possession; for he positively believed Miss Mortimer to have perished. He had obtained the documents produced before Judge Manning, at a great expense, and with considerable difficulty. What was he now to do, saddled with a wife, he, in point of fact, little cared for; he was too selfish and unprincipled to feel love for any woman beyond the hour, and the use she might hereafter be to him. His creditors were only kept back by the prospect of his inheriting Mr. Mortimer's fortune. Now there remained not a shadow of hope for him.

The appearance of Lieutenant Chamberlain, whom already he looked upon with deadly hate, rendered him furious; he set him down at once as the lover of Miss Mortimer, and vowed in his secret heart that he, at all events, should never grasp the money he considered himself entitled to. Could he have foreseen all this disappointment he would never have married Bella Calthurst.

As he left the court to reach the splendid curricle which awaited him, a man, having the features and decided look of an Israelite, pushed his way up to him, and laying his hand on his arm, said in a voice cracked with excitement and emotion, " Mein Gott! itsh gone, lost, all the money ; itsh vanished—and my ten thousand. Mein Gott ! you have robt me. I must have it."

" Have it," fiercely exclaimed Sir Herbert, dashing aside the Jew, who staggered against the railings, and laughing a horrible laugh of mockery, " To be sure you will have it when I obtain the half million you lent your four thousand upon. Two thousand in hard cash was all I had, and two thousand in rags and bones—street merchandize. Ha! ha! and for this you took my bond for ten thousand." Again he laughed, as he sprung into his curricle, and in his fury gave the spirited horses a lash they little merited.

The animals plunged madly on one side, and the pole coming in contact with a coal waggon, drawn by four horses, was smashed, and the splendid curricle became a wreck. Sir Herbert Delme was rescued from a very perilous situation between the two horses by the strong arm and desperate courage of a young man, who, grasping him by the body, lifted him out from between the plunging and kicking horses, and placed him on the pavement unhurt.

Sir Herbert cast one look up into the face of his deliverer, and then a withering curse escaped his lips, and he ground his teeth in impotent rage—his deliverer was Lieut. Chamberlain. Our hero, however, merely

observed, " You have fortunately escaped unhurt, Sir Herbert Delme. Good morning."

The baronet, livid with rage, gazed after
the young officer with a tortured heart.
" Curse him," he muttered aloud, heedless of
the crowd gathered around him.

" Hush ! hush ! for God's sake, Sir Herbert,"
whispered a young man coming up, and offer-
ing his arm; " you are hurt, and exciting
yourself."

The baronet flung off the proffered arm of
young Calthurst, with a look of disgust,
but in a moment, some new thought crossing
his mind, he immediately said—" Excuse me,
John, my fall and the smashing of my
curricle has bewildered me ; I will go with
you now." Calling his servant, he gave him
some directions respecting his carriage and
horses, and then taking John Calthurst's arm,
pushed his way haughtily through the crowd
who, as he retired, made some not very com-
plimentary remarks upon his manner and
conduct.

As they proceeded along the street, John Calthurst said, " You have hurt your foot, you limp; let me call a coach; we can then talk more unreservedly."

" Yes. I have slightly hurt my foot; that young fellow's officiousness, in what he called I suppose helping me, caused me to run greater risk of being trampled upon by those cursed horses."

A coach was called, and the two young men got in.

" Drive to Sandhurst Villa, Brompton," said John Calthurst.

" Now, then," exclaimed the baronet, with a passionate oath, as he threw himself back in the carriage, " What's to be done. Can you get me the five thousand pounds you owe me, to last me till I upset this cursed plot against my succession."

John Calthurst turned even more deadly paler, as he said bitterly, " You know very well, Herbert, that I cannot; besides, how is this a plot, if that infernal marplot of a girl exists. Of course you cannot deprive her of her right."

"But I tell you she does not exist—this fellow calling himself Lieut. Chamberlain has some scheme in view. He thinks to substitute some girl as Miss Mortimer, marry her, and claim the inheritance. This would not be so difficult a project as you imagine. There is no one in England can identify Miss Mortimer, except, perhaps, Captain Inglis, of the Cumberland packet."

"You forget," interrupted John Calthurst, "that Mrs. Cope, Miss Mortimer's mother's old attached servant, was saved and is in my father's house."

"Ah! well, that may be. I had forgotten that," returned the baronet with an oath. "You are always reminding me of something unpleasant. At all events, it is three months since this naval hero left Miss Mortimer in France. Gardner elicited, that she was dangerously ill, nearly dead when washed ashore, and when this Chamberlain escaped she was not able to leave her couch, so that it's not impossible but that she may have died. However, one thing is clear ; I must have five thousand pounds to-morrow, and you must get it, or I shall have to follow Thomas Adams to America."

" How, in the name of fate, can I get five thousand pounds," said John Calthurst. " My cursed ill luck at play sticks to me, whether I play with you as a partner or anyone else. Where's the ten thousand pounds you borrowed from Isaac Solomons ? "

Sir Herbert Delme burst into a mocking laugh. " Ten thousand pounds indeed. Did not I tell you how that bargain was made— Solomons agreed to lend me ten thousand pounds on my bond, payable twenty-one days after my coming into possession of the Mortimer's property. The old villain was sure, having seen my proofs of Annie Mortimers' death, that I was certain of the half million. I agreed to take two thousand pounds in hard cash, and two thousand in merchandise—ha! ha! merchandise—and I gave him my bond. By-the-by, I have the merchandise in a warehouse now, and I think you can turn it into cash."

" What's the merchandise, then?" demanded John Calthurst, eagerly.

" Oh, one thousand pounds in rags and bones, five hundred pounds in paving stones, and five hundred in salt herrings. These last, I am afraid, are putrid "—and the baronet laughed heartily, to the infinite disgust of John Calthurst.

" Have you," he exclaimed, "so confoundedly. Hem!—that is—did you let that usurious rascal Solomons impose such trash upon you? Why, you would not get five hundred pounds for the lot."

" Five hundred pounds," almost roared the baronet; " five hundred pence, you mean. I was only offered twenty pounds for the rags and bones, if I would cast into the bargain the paving stones and the salt herrings."

" And yet, if you had won, you would have

had to pay your bond for ten thousand pounds."

"Certainly, the two thousand pounds I did receive was the salvation of me. What should I care for the loss of eight thousand pounds out of half a million.   But drop this; you were of age nine months ago, John.   Now you must—mind, *must*—give me your acceptance at three months for five thousand pounds —I will get it cashed."

"I can't do it," said John Calthurst, "my father would turn me adrift."

"Tut, you are a fool, John," returned the baronet, snappishly, "your father took you into partnership three months ago.   He will be as liable as you will to take up your bill for five thousand pounds,—so it's all right.   Besides, you know my luck, before a month's out I will settle that sum by play. In honour, you are bound to repay me.   You have had half that sum in hard cash from me. So no more scruples, save your sister the pain of seeing me dragged off to prison, and all the chances lost of gaining the inheritance of the Mortimer's. Come, here we are,—say you agree, and not a word to Lady Delme of the result of the trial. Say it is postponed. Give me the bill, and before night we shall have funds to try our luck at the old place."

The carriage stopped; John Calthurst, a weak infatuated young man and an inveterate gambler at heart, and who felt implicit faith in Sir Herbert's wonderful luck—at last, but not without trembling, consented, and then both alighting, paid the coach, and entered the mansion where resided Lady Delme— for Sir Herbert himself resided at a fashionable hotel in ——— square, and only passed some of his spare time with his young bride in the furnished villa he rented for her at Brompton.

Lady Delme pouted and resisted at first this separation, but her husband insinuated that his time was so constantly required by his solicitor in urging forward his case, that it was imperative to reside near him—besides, until he gained his suit, it was impossible he could place her in the mansion he designed for her when that most desirable event took place.

The villa at Brompton was a small, but neatly, though not expensively, furnished house. It had a drawing-room and dining-room, three bed-rooms, and a garden front and rear, and was pleasantly situated, but had no coach-house or stable, so Sir Herbert, of course, kept his horses in town. For the first month he drove his young and really pretty bride in the park daily, took her to places of amusement, and in fact, as long as she was a novelty to him, made much of her. The second month his evenings were no longer spent at the villa; his excuse was that his lawyer was exacting, and required him at an hour that rendered it necessary for him, who was far from an early riser, to be near his office.

Though Mr. Calthurst, senior, refused to acknowledge his titled son-in-law, he did not

prevent his wife and daughter from visiting
the newly married pair. Mrs. Calthurst, to
tell the truth, furnished chiefly the sinews of
war, for though Sir Herbert Delme acquired
a small property, about six hundred a year,
by the death of his predecessor, that sum was
a mere nothing towards supplying the wilful
extravagance of the baronet, and his frequent
heavy losses in gambling.

Sir Herbert Delme, though wholly unprincipled and reckless, was still not a black
leg—he played fair ; all who knew him were
aware of that.

He frequented places high and low. When
flush of cash he was to be seen amongst titled
gamblers; for the period of our story was one
when play was lavishly indulged in by all
classes. When his funds fell, he betook himself to hells, where he mingled with the out-
casts of the gambling saloons. In one of
these last he made the acquaintance of Thomas
Adams, Mr. Calthurst's clerk, who was a
fearful victim to play. Adams had un-

fortunately inoculated John Calthurst, who easily fell into the same infatuated course.

It was about this period that Herbert Delme heard of the loss of the Cumberland packet, on board which he knew his wealthy uncle had embarked. This roused him into action, for he at once saw how useful both John Calthurst and Thomas Adams would be to him. He became introduced to Miss Bella Calthurst at his solicitor's, Mr. Gardner's, and certainly liked the young lady, and soon perceived that the best thing he could do was to secure Bella Calthurst for a wife, engage John, her brother, on his interest which he very easily managed to do, by lending him sums of money when lucky himself; this, and the young man's pride to be on intimate terms with a man who would be a baronet very shortly, completely gained him over to his side. Thomas Adams became awfully involved by his recklessness in play. One night the three were sitting after a night's carouse, at supper. Herbert Delme was boasting of the almost certainty of his succeeding to his deceased uncle's wealth. Thomas Adams accompanied him on his way to his hotel, telling him he had in important secret to impart to him.

Then it was Adams confessed to Herbert Delme that he knew Mr. Calthurst had in his charge a will executed by Mr. Mortimer, and properly witnessed; and by this will—should all Mr. Mortimer's family perish—he bequeathed the entire of his great wealth to charitable purposes, cutting off for ever Herbert Delme from the succession. This led to the abstraction of the will from Mr. Calthurst's iron chest—its destruction, and Thomas Adams's flight to America with a thousand pounds Herbert Delme raised for him, and three thousand more the unprincipled clerk managed to raise by forged cheques and bills, with Mr. Calthurst's name to them, and in all which fearful delinquencies John Calthurst became a partner.

CHAPTER VIII.

At the appointed hour Lieutenant Chamberlain proceeded to the house of Mr. Calthurst. The solicitor received his guest with the greatest kindness.

" You will excuse the absence of my family," said the solicitor; " for many reasons it would not be pleasant for you to meet them. I grieve to say my youngest daughter has made a most imprudent match. She married, without my consent or my knowledge, Sir Herbert Delme. After dinner it will be necessary that I should give you a short family history, not only of myself and family, but also of the unfortunate family of Mortimer; I can very readily imagine you are

deeply interested in the fortunes and welfare
of their daughter."

" I cordially confess to you, my dear sir,
that I am; that I have vowed to devote my
life to forward her happiness. At the same
time, I also state that I did so when in Barbadoes, and with the entire consent of Miss
Mortimer's parents. Their untimely fate
will, I am aware, be a vast impediment to
our future intercourse; for, no doubt, as soon
as Miss Mortimer reaches England, she will
become a ward in Chancery."

" Such, unquestionably, will be the case,"
said Mr. Calthurst, " but you are both very
young. Miss Mortimer is, I suppose, just
sixteen, and you are not more than twenty-
one." Our hero assented. " Therefore five
years will not make either of you exceedingly
old," and the solicitor smiled.

Our hero, in truth, did not exactly agree
with the worthy solicitor. He thought five
years an age.

" Besides," continued Mr. Calthurst, " it

does not follow that the guardians appointed
by the court will offer—I mean when they
come to understand all the circumstances of
your mutual attachment, approved of by Miss
Mortimer's parents, and your rescuing her
from an early death—I do not suppose they
will offer any objections to your union, when
she attains the more mature age of eighteen.
Ah, here is dinner. After dispatching it,
we shall understand one another better; we
shall have the evening to ourselves. My
wife, son, and daughter, are spending the day
with my imprudent child. Reconciled to
Sir Herbert Delme I never shall be; but I have
no desire to deprive his unhappy wife, for
unhappy she is, and I truly fear ever will be
as long as her unprincipled husband lives.
I leave my wife and children then to visit
and console her; for I hear he already neg-
lects her. When the time comes that he
deserts her, she will find a home here, and
every kindness and affection to solace and
screen her from trouble."

" But a change may come over Sir Herbert Delme," said our hero, "he is quite a young man; he may lead another kind of life, and repent the follies of his youth."

" If, my young friend, his acts could be called follies, we might hope; but he is steeped in vice—unprincipled, unscrupulous—and capable of any act, no matter how vile or nefarious, to carry out his aims."

After an excellent dinner, the wine and dessert on the table, the servants retired. The worthy lawyer gave the young lieutenant a brief, but perfectly clear and lucid history of the Mortimer family, and his own connection with them. Our readers are already acquainted with the particulars. Our hero then, after some comments and conversation upon what Mr. Calthurst related, gave his own brief history, and his first connection with the Mortimers, their departure from Barbadoes, and fatal capture by the " Droits de l'Homme," and the still more terrible event of the wreck and destruction. He

then gave the attentive solicitor a clear and
minute account of his and Miss Mortimer's
reception into the mansion of Monsieur de
Hauteville; the care and kindness lavished
upon the latter by Mademoiselle de Morni ;
his escape in the Fraternity, through the
connivance of Monsieur de Hauteville, and
his after adventures, till he finally reached
England.

Mr. Calthurst was amazingly surprised at
all he heard, and looked at his young guest
with undisguised admiration; his perseve-
rance, fortitude, and gallantry delighted him.
Seizing his hand, he pressed it warmly, saying,

" Upon my honour, Lieutenant Chamberlain, you richly deserve the prize you so ar-
dently desire to gain.   By your account, Miss
Mortimer is a prize in herself, and I feel satisfied that it is of her alone you think ;   her
inheritance is a very minor consideration."

" You are right, Mr. Calthurst," interrupted
the lieutenant, " on my soul.   It is her love
and her hand, I will struggle through every

difficulty and peril to obtain. If to gain this it should be necessary to forfeit her inheritance, be it so; the loss will never damp my ardent love, and, without vanity, I may say its loss will never cost Annie Mortimer a tear."

" You are young lovers," said Mr. Calthurst seriously, " and yet you have had your trials. Now I must remark to you that there is one part of your narrative somewhat mysterious and incomprehensible."

" Yes," interrupted our hero, "you allude to Monsieur de Hauteville's ambiguous conduct."

" Just so," replied the solicitor, " I cannot understand it. He gave you, apparently, a chance of escape, at the same time taking precautions to again make you a prisoner. If caught attempting escape, after giving your parole, you would have been subject to a long and rigorous confinement."

" I never gave Monsieur de Hauteville my parole; nothing of the kind was spoken of.

It was impossible to show greater kindness than he bestowed upon us."

" Is Monsieur de Hauteville a married man?" questioned Mr. Calthurst.

" No, he is a widower, has been married twice and lost both wives, after a short period, but," continued Lieutenant Chamberlain, " another thing puzzles me. Sir Herbert Delme produced in court to-day a French document signed by Captain Popatin; that statement was false. Was Captain Popatin's signature a forgery, or was the document altogether a forgery?"

" No," returned Mr. Calthurst; " the document was genuine; there was a vessel leaving Plymouth with a number of exchanged prisoners for Brest. Sir Herbert Delme made application to the authorities at Brest at the same time that I did. We both received authentic information of the death of Mr. and Mrs. Mortimer, their daughter, and infant son. But Sir Herbert, by some means or other, procured the document shown in court, which particularly referred to your's and Miss

Mortimer's death, as witnessed by this Captain Popatin. I confess I was dead beat, but your appearance changed all; and now we must set to work in earnest to obtain proof of the young lady's existence and of her present residence, and offer to ransom her, leaving the French authorities to name the amount. There is a constant exchange of prisoners, so that there will be neither difficulty nor any great delay in obtaining this intelligence."

"I trust not," said our hero. "I must visit Admiral Lord Linwood to-morrow, and then proceed to Plymouth to arrange about the prizes we took, and no doubt I shall be employed again at once, either in command of the schooner I took, as a tender to the Leander, or be appointed lieutenant to some ship in commission."

"You are right, my young friend," said Mr. Calthurst, "at your age you would be wrong to give up your profession, with such patronage as you undoubtedly have, and especially with a hot war raging—

" I would not do so on any account," returned our hero ; " I love my profession, and glory in the achievements of our gallant navy. At present I cannot assist you ; you know how to act, and I await with intense anxiety the result of your interference."

" You need not fear that either money, or exertion, or interest will be spared," said Mr. Calthurst. " To-morrow I will wait upon Lord Linwood, and put everything in train to procure Miss Mortimer's release."

Our hero left Mr. Calthurst's house, greatly pleased with the kind-hearted solicitor, and with a high opinion of his honour and integrity, and greatly regretting he had been made so unhappy by the rash marriage of his favourite daughter. On the Thursday Lieut. Chamberlain proceeded to Lord Linwood's residence at the appointed time, and was introduced into the presence of the Admiral ; his lordship had just finished his breakfast, and was attentively perusing a morning paper.

He received our hero very graciously, de-

sired him to take a chair, and then said, "I
have just been perusing a very lengthy article
upon your exploits, and upon my word, the
writer, a naval officer, who dates from Plymouth, has given you, and your crew of the
Belle Poule, a most wonderful character for
gallantry and skill. It seems, since your
escape from France, you have captured, with
a very limited crew, a schooner, a cutter, a
Spanish brig, and lastly, a remarkably handsome corvette of eighteen guns. Do you
plead guilty to these charges, Lieutenant
Chamberlain ?"

Our hero coloured to the temples, but he
modestly replied, " Very fortunate circumstances enabled me to make those captures.
As to the French corvette, she was dismasted
in a tremendous gale, and being unmanag-
able, and our schooner a remarkably fast and
easy working vessel, we were enabled to keep
out of the way of her broadside, and worried
her with a long eighteen-pound pivot gun,

when the Spanish prize brig coming to our assistance, the corvette was surrendered."

"It was a creditable thing, nevertheless, sir," said the Admiral, "and I give you credit for your gallantry. I have been thinking that this corvette should be purchased into the service. I understand it is a remarkably handsome vessel, and nearly as large as a small frigate. It is very possible it will at once be fitted out, and sent to join Commodore Nelson in the Mediterranean. It is unfortunate that you are so young, and your service as a lieutenant so short. You belong to the Leander now, but I shall so arrange that you take this corvette out, and on joining Nelson's fleet you will take the berth of second lieutenant to the Leander, and surrender the corvette, which shall be named the Surprise, to the Honourable St. George Forester, who has just been made a commander. He is now in Lord Nelson's ship, the Vanguard."

At the mention of St. George Forester, our hero slightly started; that was the name which had caused the young lady he had seen on his first visit so much emotion.

"Does this arrangement suit your wishes, Mr. Chamberlain?" continued Lord Linwood.

"It is more than I could possibly either hope for or expect, my lord," returned our hero. "Pardon me, may I request a favour for a very gallant and skilful officer. He has served in the navy as master's mate, was on board the Fox privateer when taken by the Belle Poule, and in the two engagements that followed greatly contributed to my success. He wishes to re-enter the service and serve in the same ship with myself."

"Well," returned the Admiral, after a moment's thought, "give me his name; he can go out with you in the corvette, and shall receive an appointment as master's mate on board the Leander; that will be a step, the Leander being a fifty-gun ship."

Our hero expressed himself exceedingly

grateful; in fact he felt considerable surprise at the favour shown him by Lord Linwood.

"The corvette," remarked Lord Linwood, as our hero was taking his leave, "will not be ready for sea for a fortnight, as she is thoroughly re-fitting, and having heavier guns put on board. I dare say you will be able to get many of the men who served with you in the Belle Poule to re-enter the service, and sail in the corvette."

"They will be glad to do so, my lord," said Lieutenant Chamberlain, "I have no doubt," and he took his leave. Though his appointment as second lieutenant of the Leander was a most flattering one for one so young, and opened out so favourable a career; still, he would, somehow, rather have retained the command of the Belle Poule, as a tender to the Leander. However, he seemed, as far as his career in the service went, to have been an especial favourite with fortune; therefore he would not be so ungrateful as to find fault with her favours. As he de-

scended the stairs, immersed in thought, and
was crossing the hall, a smart, pretty girl,
attired like a lady's maid, stopped him, and
requested him to follow her. Surprised as
our hero was, he nevertheless obeyed her be-
hest.   Passing out of the hall, they entered a
wide passage, which led to another part of the
house.   Here she stopped, and threw open a
door, saying, " Please to walk into this room,
sir."

The young sailor's face flushed, as he
stepped into a room looking very like a
housekeeper's apartment. Seated at a table,
with books, keys, and small boxes, was an old
lady, dressed in black silk, a neat cap on her
head, and a pair of silver spectacles on a remarkably high nose. " It's strange," thought
our hero, " who's this?"

" Pray take a chair, sir," said the old lady,
rising and putting one forward.

A little mystified and curious, he sat down,
and was going to speak, but his companion
interrupted him. " Excuse me, sir, I am quite

deaf, and can only hear with my trumpet, and I will not trouble you with such an instrument. Miss Flora will be here directly," and she resumed her totting up of a very formidable-looking account in one of her books.

"Miss Flora," muttered our hero, "who's Miss Flora?" He had not much time for thought, for the door opened, and the same beautiful girl he had seen on his first visit entered the room, closing the door after her.

The gentleman rose, and saluted the lady with great respect; with a heightened colour she returned the salutation, and then, with a sweet smile, said, pointing to a chair at the further end of the room, "You will not think my conduct strange, Mr. Chamberlain, when I give you an explanation. Though strangers to each other," she added, in a soft, pleasing tone, "we are nevertheless very near relatives."

The person addressed looked amazed, but most highly interested, and the girl continued,

" You must, I suppose, when a boy, have heard your mother's name mentioned ? "

" Yes," returned our hero, "I always understood that her maiden name was Elphinstone —Ellen Maud Elphinstone."

" Yes," said the young girl, with a sigh, " your mother and mine were sisters."

" Is it possible ! " exclaimed our hero, with delighted surprise, " then we are first cousins, and I—I, who really did not think I had a relative in the world, now find I have a most charming one. Look upon me," added our hero, warmly, " as a brother, and do not hesitate to tax our connection to the uttermost, if I can serve you."

" Thank you, cousin. You cannot imagine how gladly I claim the relationship. I did not know it myself yesterday ; but I must be brief in what I have to say, for my aunt may at any moment return, and when she does, she will expect my presence."

" Who is your aunt, and by what name shall I remember you ? "

"My name is Flora Smith—a name that created all my mother's misfortunes, and is causing mine. You do not know," she continued, " that Lord Linwood is your uncle?— and the lady you saw yesterday is our aunt, Lord Linwood's sister?"

"You amaze me; but it accounts for his conduct, which I thought much too gracious in my reception for a poor lieutenant."

" Then he did not acknowledge you for his nephew?" asked Flora.

" No," replied our hero, " not a word likely to lead to such a supposition passed between us. I was not aware that Lord Linwood's name was Elphinstone—I know so little of my family history or connections. I was only eight years old when I became an orphan. We do not enquire much about connections at that age; and before I was thirteen I was sent to sea. I remember being told by a Mrs. Talbot, with whom I passed all my vacations—and very happy days they were, for she was a most motherly and kind woman—she said, as she embraced me, before my departure for sea, ' Remember, my dear boy, your mother was an Elphinstone.' But the exciting life I have led from that day to this has left little time for thought or reflection."

" Well, my dear cousin," went on Flora, " I can only briefly tell you how your mother and mine came to be so cruelly neglected by our high connections. The late Earl of Linwood had three daughters and two sons. There was not a prouder or more imperious man in England than our grandfather. His pride was such that he rendered himself wretched from the intense fear that one or other of his daughters should make a match derogatory to her station as an earl's daughter. They were therefore kept in great seclusion till they should attain their eighteenth year. I have no time for particulars—it will be sufficient to say, that Lady Ellen Elphinstone, your mother, the youngest of the three sisters, eloped with the young and high-spirited

Lieutenant Chamberlain, considered one of the handsomest officers in the service. The rage and fury of the earl may be imagined. He repudiated his daughter—even cursed her in his wrath—and forbade her name ever to be mentioned in his presence. He endeavoured to get your father out of the service, but in vain ; though he marred his fortunes, and had him sent on a foreign and unhealthy station. Your mother died in giving you birth, and your father, a proud and high-spirited man, never would allow his wife's relations and connections to be named in his presence. The second daughter, Flora Maud Elphinstone, was more strictly guarded, and, shortly after her sister's elopement, was told that she was to give her hand to a nobleman, old enough to be her father. At that time she was re-siding in the family mansion in Shropshire. The eldest sister, the counter part of her father, was married to Lord Edgehill, who, after many years, died, leaving her a widow, and his estates deeply involved.

My mother, as I said before, lived in Shrop-shire, under the guardianship of a maiden lady of the name of Coulsten. In six months she was to be married. An accident, how-ever, or else the will of Providence, upset all the earl's plans and projects; it seemed as if his pride was to be humbled through his daughters' disobedience.

" The agent of the earl's estates in Shrop-shire was an attorney of the name of Smith; a man of humble birth, but highly respectable as to character and conduct. He had an only son—a very handsome and talented young man, educated for the bar. He chanced to come down to Hamstead Manor on pressing business. That night Mrs. Coulsten, who had a habit of reading in bed, set fire to her curtains. Flora Elphin-stone slept in a room that communicated with Mrs. Coulsten's. Awoke by the flames and the scorching heat, Mrs. Coulsten jumped from her bed, and rushed, in her fear and abstraction, into Lady Flora's bed-chamber.

The flames spread through both rooms; and though the alarm was soon conveyed all over the mansion, there is very little doubt but the two ladies would have perished, had not young Albert Smith burst through the flames, gained their room, and lowered them, one after the other, from the window into the garden, by uniting the sheets and blankets, also escaping himself in the same manner.

" Luckily only one wing of the mansion of Hamstead was destroyed, but that terrible event led to another ; Lady Flora fell in love with her deliverer, and he with her. Love laughs at distinctions; my mother cared little about becoming Mrs. Smith; so, following your mother's example, she eloped with her lover, went to Scotland, and was married.

" Here was a second blow to the proud earl. A daughter of his married to an attorney's son, and of the name of Smith!"

Just at this part of the narrative the lady's maid put her head in at the door, saying,

" Quick, Miss Flora, your aunt's carriage is at the door."

" Ah !" exclaimed Flora, changing colour, " so soon, and I so much to say. Tell me, cousin, where I can direct a letter to you, that you will be sure to get."

" Write to me, and direct, ' Care of Mrs. Penson, Woodbine Cottage, Elm Tree Road, Chelsea,' that's where my second mother and her daughter live."

An uproar of bells throughout the mansion started Flora off like a frightened deer; kissing her hand, and pressing it affectionately, our hero bade her adieu, Flora having merely time to say, " My maid will show you the way out; but not through the front door." The next instant he was alone with the deaf housekeeper, whom he perceived was still quietly occupied with her grand totals, not even looking up from her books. In a few minutes Phœbe, Flora's maid, returned. She looked up demurely into the handsome face of the lieutenant, saying, " Now sir, if you please, I will show you the way out."

" Thank you," returned our hero, " I am ready." As they passed the housekeeper she looked up, nodded her head, saying, three hundred and seventy nine pounds, fourteen shillings, and eightpence three farthings; that's the total. Next moment they were in the passage. Our hero bowed politely, and followed the girl.

" Ah !" said Phœbe, as she stopped and opened a door, and let her bright eyes rest upon her companion, " You think the old lady deaf, eh?"

" Why, yes, I should think so," said our hero, slipping a guinea into the hand of the very pretty lady's maid, who smiled, and looked as if she would have preferred being paid by a more sterling coin ; but our hero was a true lover, and although sailors are proverbially rather partial to ruby lips, Phœbe's escaped contact.

" Why do you ask me if I think the old

dame is deaf?" said our hero, as Phœbe opened the door.

" Because," said the girl, " she hears as well as I do. She's Miss Flora's friend ; but there are many secrets in this great house. You are not my young lady's lover, are you?"—and she looked very inquisitive.

" No, I am not. I dare say your young mistress will tell you who I am.''

" Don't be afraid of me, sir," said the girl, "for I would go through fire and water for Miss Flora." She then added, " just cross the yard, sir, open the door you see yonder, and you will be in a lane ; turn to your left, and it will lead you into Grosvenor Street."

Our hero passed across the wide court, and had just put his hand up to lift the latch, when the door opened, and he stood face to face with a tall, strapping footman, with a powdered wig, and scarlet plush breeches.

"Ah ! curse me, if this isn't too bad," said the man, his face flushing, " I've caught you ; so this is the way you come prowling after that treacherous little devil, Phœbe,"—and he doubled his fists menacingly.

" My good fellow, you are quite mistaken," said the lieutenant, inclined to laugh. "Here's a crown to drink his Majesty's health. So move from the door way."

" Curse you, and his—hem—I mean the crown. I want none of your money. I'll smash in your *crown*, if I don't my name's not Thomas."

" Ah !" said the lieutenant, warding off a desperate blow of the admirer of Phœbe, who was in a state of savage excitement. The next moment the unfortunate, jealous lover found himself prostrate in the yard, his legs in the air, and his hat, cane, and wig scattered on the flags.

Thomas was astounded; as he struggled up on his legs his eyes rested upon the head of Phœbe protruded through the open door, making signs to him to come to her quick.

" Ah, treacherous little jade ; I'll pay you for all this, and that puppy that's sneaking here after you, there must have been two of them. Some fellow tripped me up, whilst the other must have hit me a buster in the bread-basket. Curse him, it was a smeller, no doubt;" and he rubbed his head, picked up his wig, and walked up to Phœbe, wishing to pour forth his wrath. But Phœbe was the first to begin.

" Here's a pretty mess you have made, Thomas, to attempt to strike the Austrian Ambassador's Secretary, the Count de Hatchengrotzen whom I was purposely ordered, in secret, to let out by the back door, whilst the Danish Ambassador came in by the front. I tremble to think of it; you may bring on a war with those two powers by your conduct."

Thomas stood aghast.

" What," said he, " was that young man the—"

" Ambassador's nephew, I told you. But don't look frightened. If you keep the secret, he will; but it's dreadful to think what might happen. I thought, Thomas, I had put you up to some of the secrets of this house, but I hope you're not hurt; bless me, he tumbled you over like a nine-pin—and you such a stout able fellow."

" I slipped, Phœbe, and fell just as he was rushing past," said Thomas, regaining his colour; "but, indeed, Phœbe, I thought he was one of those puppies who frequent the square, trying to get a glimpse of you"—

"Of me, indeed," said Phœbe, with a look of great contempt, " I beg, Thomas, you will not insult me by such insinuations, or else you and—"

" Well, well—pray forgive me, Phœbe—I was only making an excuse for my folly, so pray forget and forgive."

" Well, there's my hand, I forgive you."

Thomas kissed the hand extended to him, and Phœbe proceeded along the passage with quite a dignified air, followed by Thomas, who

was regarding his plushes with a sorrowful
look, they having sustained considerable injury
by his roll over a pool of muddy water which
a broken flag had collected in the yard.

CHAPTER VII.

AMAZINGLY surprised at the disclosures made to him by his pretty and interesting cousin, our hero, after leaving the discomfited Thomas Dooley, passed out of the lane, and soon found himself in Grosvenor-street. He considered for a while what he should do for the rest of the day, till he recollected that there was still time to pay a visit to Chelsea, provided he got a hackney coach to expedite his movements. After proceeding through two or three streets, he engaged one, and told the man to drive him to the entrance of Elm-tree-road, Chelsea.   As far as time was concerned, the lieutenant found that he might just as well have made use of his legs. However, having arrived there, he paid and dismissed the lumbering coach of sixty odd years ago, and then proceeded along the row of cottages with their gardens running down to the river. Eight eventful years had passed since he left Woodbine Cottage, a mere boy, and became a midshipman, to fight his way in the world, and as he often thought in the solitary hours of his watch, without a friend or relative to care whether he perished or lived. In those eight years he had gained many friends amongst his comrades, and in the ranks of his superiors. He had passed his examination with great credit; had been otherwise fortunate, for he had gained the love of a beautiful and amiable girl, and with the consent of her parents, though she was an heiress worth thousands, and he only a poor lieutenant. On his return to England, he suddenly found himself, at two-and twenty, made a full lieutenant; and, more extraordinary still, instead of being without a relative, he could claim a peer of the realm as an uncle, and a young and lovely girl as a cousin.

It all appeared to him a dream; and he become so absorbed in thought that he was actually passing Woodbine Cottage, when an exclamation from a female voice startled him out of his day-dreams. Looking round, he beheld Rose Talbot standing at the little gate of the cottage.

" Ah, Rose," exclaimed our hero, hastening back ; and, taking both the girl's hands, he pressed a brotherly kiss on her glowing cheeks, " What a reverie I was in. Coming to the well-remembered cottage, and seeing neither it, nor the fair occupant. But how is your dear mother. Rose, I am so glad to see you, you can't think; we parted in such a strange way."

" Ah ! Augustus, if our missing each other caused you trouble, you can fancy what anxiety it cost us. How rejoiced my mother will be to see you !"

Mrs. Penson, who saw the meeting from

the window, rushed out to meet them, throwing her arms round our hero's neck, and kissing him with the affection of a mother.

All three talking at the same time, so rejoiced were they to see each other, entered the neat and tastefully furnished parlour.

" Ah!" said our hero, looking round the room, and recognising many a well-remembered object. "I can fancy myself a boy again, and could have a game of romps with you, Rose, like old times."

" Ah, the dear old times!" said the girl, gazing with a bright tear glistening in her eyes, into the handsome, animated features of the athletic sailor. " I can scarcely believe, Augustus, that you were once the light, active, curly-haired boy, that used to climb the old cedars like a squirrel, and hang by the branches to frighten me to death."

" And you, my little Rose, have sprung into a blooming girl. Time, old Time—what eight years can do!"

" Shortly after, the happy party sat down

to a modest, but well-dressed dinner. They
all had so much to say that they scarcely
thought of eating; but when seated round the
cheerful blaze of a sea-coal fire, our hero said,
"Now, dear mother, I have a hundred questions to ask, and a great deal to tell you, but
there is one uppermost in my mind. Where
is my esteemed friend Hawkins, and how is
he? I had not five minutes to spare at
Plymouth to make enquiries, being the bearer
of important despatches for the Admiralty."

"Ah! poor fellow," said Mrs. Penson,
"how he chafed and fretted when we parted
company. He was here a week ago, and I
fully expect he will be here the day after
to-morrow. He's quite well, but very anxious
to see you."

"Yes," said Rose. "We had a rough
passage across. In the night, or just before
it became dark, in a squall, all the rigging
slipped over the mast-head so hastily made,
and down came all the sails, and before anything could be done, we almost drifted on

shore, and nearly rolled the mast out. Then came the fog and snowstorm. Our good friend Hawkins was afraid to carry sail, our rigging had been badly put up during the night, and we had drifted greatly to lee-ward; but getting at last a lull in the gale, he strengthened his rigging, and the wind shifting, he bore away, and after a stormy passage, we succeeded in making Plymouth."

Our hero related to his interested listeners his adventures from the period of their sepa-ration till he came to England. He did not say a word, however, of what had passed between him and Lord Linwood, for he wished to ask Mrs. Penson a few questions first.

Mother and daughter were greatly as-tonished and delighted at his good fortune in capturing such rich prizes.

"How pleased," said Rose, "Mr. Hawkins will be. You will be rich, dear Augustus, and all by your own gallantry."

"Yes," added her mother; "and no thanks to his proud relations, who cruelly and sternly forbade any intercourse."

"My dear adopted mother," said Lieutenant Chamberlain, "you have now, for the first time, mentioned my relatives. I was going to speak to you on that very subject. When I arrived in England, five or six days ago, I did not know I had a relative in existence, and behold I have found an uncle and aunt and, in truth, a most charming cousin in a very interesting girl."

"Is it possible?" exclaimed Mrs. Penson, surprised. "I knew your dear mother's name, and that she was the daughter, the youngest daughter of a lord, who cruelly cursed her for marrying a poor lieutenant in the navy. But I have never heard anything more of the family. I never mixed with great people, and knew little about them. Your poor father could never bear to hear your mother's family spoken of, for her father's harshness preyed upon her mind. So, my dear boy," added Mrs. Penson, "you have discovered all about them. How was it, my dear?"

Our hero related his introduction to Admiral Lord Linwood, and spoke of his very gracious reception, and also his promise of getting him appointed second lieutenant of the Leander, and said he was to take out to the Mediterranean the French corvette he had captured.

Mother and daughter were in truth greatly delighted at our hero's prospects. "Do you know," said Mrs. Penson, "I think I can tell you who the pretended deaf housekeeper is?"

"Who is she?" exclaimed the lieutenant, much interested.

"I will tell you," answered Mrs. Penson. "Your dear mother used often to speak in terms of affection of her. She nursed her and her sister. Her name is Susan Hopeton. I am sure it is she. But did not Lord Linwood seem to know that you were his nephew? Surely, being aware that you were the son of

Captain Chamberlain, the truth must have struck him."

"If he did know, he said nothing; but I certainly think I owe my advance in rank in the service to being his nephew. I heard rumours when in Plymouth that the present ministers would go out on a certain question that was to come before the House, and that the opposition had a great majority ; so probably, knowing I was his nephew, he made use of his *influence* to advance me in rank. Some of my brother officers, who have no doubt seen more service, may envy me."

"Indeed, dear Augustus," remarked Rose, "I cannot see or understand why they should envy you what you have so bravely earned."

"I have an able friend in you, Rose," returned her friend smiling, "by-the-by, if Miss Flora Smith writes to me she will direct her letters here. I fancy her family wish to marry the poor girl to some one she does not love. She mentioned the first lieutenant of the £——to me, the Honourable St. George

Forester; he is nearly as young a man as I am, and is next heir to a peerage. I begin to see into the cause of Flora's troubles, she doubtless loves one, perhaps another neither gifted by fortune nor blessed with rank. What a strange destiny has prevailed over the daughters of the house of Linwood. All acting contrary to the wishes and intentions of their relations and guardians."

" And why not, Augustus," cried Rose, with animation, " we cannot always control the feelings of our hearts. Women's affections are not to be forced into channels laid down for them. Who can say why a woman loves, or why she selects the object of her choice from amongst those least likely to please her guardians."

" Very true, my little Rose," said our hero, " we can none of us, male or female, control our affections. Love is a spontaneous feeling, and in some hearts becomes so strong as to overpower all others. But I must be moving; it is getting late, and I do not know what

may be the order of the day for to-morrow.
I shall have to leave England before any
tidings from France can reach me, and you
can fancy my anxiety with respect to Miss
Mortimer."

"Yes," said Mrs. Penson, "You must be
anxious. However, when you left her she
was getting rapidly well, after the terrible
trials the dear girl had endured."

"She was out of danger, certainly," replied
the lieutenant, "but there is something in her
situation under the roof of the Chateau de
Hauteville that mystifies and perplexes me;
and till Mr. Calthurst obtains more certain
information I must remain uneasy and un-
comfortable."

Rose Talbot could easily perceive that
Augustus Chamberlain's affection for Miss
Mortimer was likely to become, if it were not
so already, the ruling passion of his heart.
Women are quicker in coming to a conclusion
in affairs of the heart than men. Rose had
her own thoughts and ideas on the subject,

but she kept them to herself.   Taking a most affectionate leave of mother and daughter, and promising to return on Thursday, he bade them good night, and hailing a hackney coach, returned to his hotel.

Immediately after breakfast the following morning, being anxious to see Mr. Calthurst he procceded to his office. As he passed along the hall leading to the different rooms he came face to face with Mr. John Calthurst. As the solicitor's son looked up into the lieutenant's face, his own cheek flushed and his manner became agitated and confused. Our hero knew he was the solicitor's son, and therefore l owed politely. John Calthurst appeared to hesitate, but the next instant said, " Mr. Chamberlain, may I request five minutes' conversation with you."

" Certainly," returned the lieutenant quietly, though a little surprised.

John Calthurst led the way into a small but neatly furnished room, and closing the door carefully, turned round and faced his visitor.

The ghastly expression of his countenance forcibly struck our hero; in fact, thinking he was fainting, he caught him by the arm, saying, "what is the matter, Mr. Calthurst, you appear agitated; do not be afraid to trust me. If you are in trouble depend on it I will help you if I can."

The young man sunk into a chair; the perspiration standing in drops upon his forehead, but making a great effort, he said, in a somewhat unsteady voice, "Mr. Chamberlain, I am about to request of you a favour— one which I can scarcely hope you will grant. I have no right to expect it. However, if you refuse me, I am a ruined man, and shall before twenty-four hours are over stand before the world a convicted forger." The youth trembled so that his chair shook under him—a pitiable object to behold.

"I am extremely shocked," Lieutenant Chamberlain said. "What have you done, Mr. Calthurst. Say, quickly, what can I do to screen you from such a miserable position."

"I wish to save my father from cursing his infatuated son," said John Calthurst, recovering his firmness. " To do this, I require a thousand pounds before four o'clock to day. If I threw myself at my father's feet, and confessed all, he would save me from the terrible doom hanging over me ; but he would never see me again—his kind and honourable heart would be crushed."

" Say no more," said our hero, "give me pen and ink," and as he spoke he took a pocket-book from his breast. John Calthurst, with eager but trembling hands took pens and ink from a writing desk, and placed them before Lieutenant Chamberlain, who tearing a leaf from his book, wrote a cheque for a thousand pounds, and handing it to John Calthurst said, " Take this to Messrs. Milsom and Co., bankers, Leadenhall-street, and the amount will be paid you—lose no time, and try and recover your nerve."

The unfortunate young man's eyes became suffused with tears, which however served to relieve him. He pressed our hero's hand to his lips, saying "Your generosity will save me. I need not request you to keep this affair secret. I can repay you in time, and from this hour, as long as life is spared me, I will never touch card or dice, or enter a gambling-house, or associate with those who have made me what I am. I will pray to God to forgive me, and endeavour by repentance and leading a new life, to regain the esteem of my father, who, I know, suspects me of being misled; but, thank God, he thinks me incapable of committing the crime, that indubitably would have led me to the gallows;" and again taking our hero's hand, he pressed it to his lips with passionate energy, and rushed from the room.

"Well," thought our hero, "I hope that is a thousand pounds well laid out. I can imagine how this has occurred. I'm not very rich, but if this escape from detected crime and its punishment changes this young man's mode of life, the money will be very well expended." So thinking, he found his way to the office, and from thence to Mr. Calthurst's private room.

The solicitor received our hero most cordially; he seemed, nevertheless, very serious, and was busy looking over some law papers. As our hero seated himself, Mr. Calthurst said, " I have forwarded all the necessary papers and information respecting Miss Mortimer, to my correspondent in Plymouth. An exchange of prisoners takes place soon. In five days the vessel leaves with a cartel for Brest, and my friend is to send a clever and keen agent in the vessel, to carry out our object, so that in eight or ten days we may expect to receive satisfactory intelligence. We have left the French authorities to fix the ransom for Miss Mortimer."

" I am rejoiced," said Lieutenant Chamberlain, "that I have every chance of remaining in England for a fortnight, or perhaps more, and I shall be able to hear the result of your application to the French Go-

veinment. Miss Mortimer, not being a
prisoner of war, and having been cast upon
the coast of France by shipwreck, will make
a vast difference; besides, I have heard that
the French Government treated Captain
Inglis, of the Cumberland, and all persons
saved from the wrecks of the Droits and the
Amazon with great kindness and courtesy."

"Very much so," said Mr. Calthurst.

"I wish, Mr. Calthurst," said our hero,
"that you would be kind enough to take
charge of whatever cash I may receive
as my share of prize-money. It will
amount to a pretty tolerable sum, and also
what remains of the little fortune saved
for me by my poor dear father, which I will
place in your hands to-morrow; you will
do the best you can with it, and when I
want cash I will draw upon you, if you permit will me."

"I shall be most happy, my dear sir, to do
everything I can to meet your wishes. I trust
in a few years to see you united to the object of

your choice, and when that takes place you will be one of the wealthiest men in England."

"Let me only know that the dear girl to whom I have plighted my troth is once more on the soil of old England, and it's very little concern her wealth would give me."

"Ah!" said the solicitor, with a smile, "you sailors are proverbially careless as to wealth."

Lieut. Chamberlain laughed, saying, "to have and to spend is generally our motto— our mode of life no doubt causes this apparent recklessness of money."

"How did your interview with Admiral Lord Linwood terminate?" questioned the solicitor.

"Oh! beyond my most sanguine wishes," returned our hero, relating the result of the interview.

"You surprise me," returned Mr. Calthurst, "for I know something of Lord Linwood, whose stern and severe nature is seldom won upon. He is known to be the strictest disciplinarian, and almost incapable of rewarding merit alone—I sincerely congratulate you on your prospects, though your success, notwithstanding your gallantry and merit, still astonishes me."

"Ah," said Lieut. Chamberlain, with a smile, "your surprise will cease when I tell you Lord Linwood is my uncle."

" Your uncle," returned the solicitor, " you amaze me still more. Lord Linwood is considered to be without an heir—the title dies with him. If you are his nephew, you must be the heir to the title and estates; his two wives died without leaving him a child— male or female. His elder brother, the earl, never married, is twelve years older than his brother. and in very infirm health."

" My mother," said our hero, " was Lady Ellen Elphinstone, youngest daughter of the deceased earl; her elder sister Flora married a Mr. Smith; he died, leaving an only daughter, now dwelling in the mansion of

Lord Linwood, and a very beautiful and interesting young girl she is."

"Well, upon my word," said Mr. Calthurst, "you bewilder me. I always understood that two of the daughters of the late Earl of Linwood had eloped, made disreputable matches, and died neglected and disowned by their relatives. Whereas one, you say, married your father, an officer, and of an exceedingly respectable family—no better name in all Wiltshire."

"I am ignorant, my dear sir, of my family history or connections," said our hero, "but I heard last night, from good authority, that, so enraged were the Linwoods at my mother's marriage with my father, they not only disowned my mother, but did everything in their power to drive my father from the navy, and when they failed, he was sent for years to a foreign and an unhealthy station. My father, a proud and honourable man, cared nothing about his wife's connections ; never spoke of them, so that at his death all remembrance of my mother's family dropped into oblivion."

"Nevertheless, my dear sir," said the solicitor, "you are the next male heir to the title and estates, and your uncle must have known it when he heard your name ; and yet you say he never hinted at your relationship."

"Not in the least; he was gracious enough, but treated me as a perfect stranger. Probably he waits till I gain further fame or perish."

"I tell you what we must do," said the solicitor, after a moment's consideration, " we must find out where your father was married. You, of course, do not know, and I suppose, never enquired.   Did he leave no papers, letters, or documents behind him ?"

"I cannot say," returned Lieut. Chamberlain, "but I think Captain Thompson, of the Leander, or Mrs. Penson, who resides at Chelsea, and whom I saw last night, and whose first husband was a most attached, though humble, friend of my father, knows something about it ; at all events, I can enquire. I am not ambitious," continued our hero, " but the knowledge that I could claim Lord Linwood as my uncle, might have a great influence on the guardians who may hereafter be appointed to take care of Miss Mortimer and her fortune."

" Decidedly so," returned Mr. Calthurst, "your pretensions to Miss Mortimer's hand could never be objected to."

" You met my son as you came along the passage," said Mr. Calthurst, after the conversation on our hero's affairs had ceased.

" Yes," returned our hero, quietly, " I have not had the pleasure of being introduced to him, but I recognised him, having seen him in the court the other day."

" I am very uneasy respecting him," said Mr. Calthurst, seriously, " I do not think he is naturally inclined to vicious pursuits; but since his intimacy with Sir Herbert Delme I have observed a terrible change in his manner

and looks. I know he plays, and has probably
lost the handsome allowance I make him, and
has got in debt—no doubt to his precious
friend Sir Herbert.   If that is all, I am
willing to help him on a solemn assertion
that he has committed no crime, or any way
involved the honour of our house.   Pray,
my dear sir," added the solicitor, "did he
speak to you on the subject? For I heard you
both turn back from the door; I recognized
your voice saying good morning."

This was an unpleasant question for
our hero to answer, and he really felt
himself in a fix, when the door suddenly
opened, and a clerk said, popping in his
head, "Sir Herbert Delme, sir, insists upon
seeing you for five minutes." Mr. Calthurst
looked angry; but before he could say a
word, the clerk was thrust aside, and the
baronet entered the office, his face flushed
and his manner excited. He paused as his
eyes rested upon Lieutenant Chamberlain,
and a dark malignant scrowl crossed his

brows. Our hero looked him calmly in the face; there was no mistaking the hostile expression of the baronet's countenance; but, taking no notice of it, he took up his hat, and, shaking hands with the greatly annoyed solicitor, passed out of the office.

CHAPTER X.

After Mr. Chamberlain's departure from the solicitor's office, Sir Herbert Delme threw himself into a chair, and regarded his father-in-law almost savagely.

Mr. Calthurst, with an effort, recovered his composure, and, looking at the baronet, said, calmly, " I thought, Sir Herbert Delme, that after what has passed, all intercourse between our families had ceased. Pray, what is the purport of your visit?"

The baronet, with a sneer upon his lip, took out his pocket-book, and selected from its leaves a folded paper. " Whatever, sir, your feelings are towards me, the husband of your daughter, I do not come to inquire. But your son John owes me the sum of five thousand pounds." Mr. Calthurst gave a slight start. "For payment he handed me his bill for thirty-one days. Before I pass this bill, which I must do this day, I thought it but right to ask you, as you have taken your son into partnership, whether you will pay it when presented at your banker's."

"Such a debt as five thousand pounds," said Mr. Calthurst, quietly, "could only have been incurred, by a young man just of age, in reckless gambling in disreputable places. If he can take up his bill, and chooses to do so, well and good. I do not hold myself responsible for his infatuation or disgraceful gambling debts."

Sir Herbert Delme smiled a scornful, bitter smile as he quietly returned the bill to his pocket-book.

"Very good, sir. You have given me an answer. I must now tell you that your decision will unquestionably hang your son."

"What do you mean?" exclaimed Mr.
Calthurst, starting from his chair, his features
betraying considerable agitation. "I suspect
my son has been cruelly and wickedly misled, and that he may have involved himself;
but committing crime is another thing. What,
therefore, do you mean by such words as you
have uttered?"

"Simply," returned Sir Herbert, looking
at his watch, a smile of triumph on his lip,
"that your son has passed a bill for five
thousand pounds to one Jacob Jacob, the
broker, that this bill purports to be drawn
by you, and bears your signature."

Mr. Calthurst sank back into his chair,
powerless and pale as death, the hand resting
on the table, trembling with overpowering
emotion, whilst the baronet seemed to enjoy
the solicitor's agony.

"To you, the husband of my daughter,"
said Mr. Calthurst, "I owe the ruin and misery
of my whole family." By a tremendous effort
he had recovered his nerve. "If what you

say is true, my son has disgraced himself; but he cannot, by simply putting my name to a bill, be accused of forgery ; for, of course, when the bill is presented, it will be paid without question or remark. If Jacob Jacob possesses such a bill, I will take it up at once. Now," continued the solicitor, " what is your real object in coming here? for by telling me this guilty act of my son, you appear to me to defeat your own purpose, if that purpose was to extort money."

" I shall wish you good morning, Mr. Calthurst," returned the baronet, quite coolly, " my object is answered. I need not trespass further on your valuable time." So, taking up his hat, he was walking towards the door, when it was thrown open, and John Calthurst, heated and excited, hastily entered the office. The young man looked at Sir Herbert with a glance of unmitigated disgust and anger.

" You are before me, I see, Sir Herbert Delme," said John Calthurst, bitterly; "having tried to destroy me in the eyes of the world, you come to poison the ears of my father, by stating to him his son's madness, infatuation, and crimes. You may make him wretched; but you have, thank God, failed in driving me to ruin."

"There, sir," continued John Calthurst, placing before his astounded and bewildered father a bill of exchange, with his signature to it—a bill for five thousand pounds—drawn at sight, and payable at Burden, Fife and Co's., bankers, Pall Mall.

The solicitor, with a shudder, took up the bill, and tore it to fragments.

"Well, gentlemen," said the baronet, his face livid with rage, but still suppressing his passion, "I am *de trop* in this little family scene, and having nothing more to say I will leave you to become reconciled," and, fixing his eyes upon John Calthurst, he said, his rage getting the better of him, "you, John Calthurst, weak, shuffling, contemptible as I know you to be, take care, and do not cross my path, or you will rue the doing so.

As to your daughter, sir," turning his dark glance upon Mr. Calthurst, "you may take her home if you like—from this time I discard her."

"She will live to bless you, Sir Herbert, for this determination, which I always anticipated," said the solicitor, coolly. "She will return to her home a wiser and, I hope, a better woman."

"Very possibly," returned the baronet, savagely; "but please to remember, Mr. John Calthurst, that I hold your bill for five thousand pounds, which becomes due in a few days, and, depend on it, I will enforce payment."

"You had better remember, Sir Herbert Delme," said John Calthurst, "before you present that bill for payment, that the will stolen by Thomas Adams, and for which you paid him one thousand pounds, is in my possession."

Sir Herbert Delme became rooted to the spot on which he stood, whilst Mr. Calthurst

uttered an exclamation of horror and astonishment—then a feeling of intense relief
pervaded his mind, though he inwardly shuddered when the thought crossed his mind that
his son was mixed up, if not a partner in
crime, with Sir Herbert Delme and Thomas
Adams.

" John Calthurst," said the baronet, in a
voice that seemed to be hissed through his
teeth, " for one so young, you are a most des-
picable, cowardly villain."

" Yes," returned the young man, pale and
haggard with the feelings that rent his breast,
" Yes, I am; but who made me so—you—till
I met you I was, at all events, innocent of
crime. But respecting the robbery of this
will by Adams—you know I knew nothing of
it till after it was effected—concealing the
knowledge I accidentally gained was bad
enough. How I obtained the will you thought
destroyed I shall not state; the will, I feel
satisfied, will be of no consequence, as Miss
Mortimer lives."

"Stay one moment; let me speak," said Mr. Calthurst, who appeared to be suffering greatly. "All you have uttered said is horrible to listen to. You, Sir Herbert Delme, are my daughter's husband; you will hereafter lead a separate life, but let us keep this terrible amount of crime to ourselves. You hold my son's acceptance for five thousand pounds—no matter how you obtained it, or how he became your debtor for that sum—give it to me, and here is a cheque for the amount on Messrs. Burden, Fife and Co. For your own sake, I have no doubt, all that has passed will be forgotten. My son shall go abroad for a year or two; and I trust that you, Sir Herbert, will see that the path of crime is a crooked one, and that there is no villany, however well concocted, but meets its punishment, and that when least expected."

Sir Herbert Delme listened with perfect composure to the solicitor's words, which appeared to have no other effect than to restore him to his usual self-possession—for he coolly took out John Calthurst's acceptance, and placed it on the table, whilst Mr. Calthurst having drawn a cheque, handed it to the baronet, who quietly placed it in his pocket-book, saying—

" I beg you to understand, Mr. Calthurst, that what has passed between ourselves shall go no further, of that be satisfied; but, at the same time, permit me to say I shall take steps to dispute Mr. Mortimer's will, that is if Miss Mortimer has ceased to exist. I have every reason to suppose Thomas Adams has deceived us all, and that the paper Mr. John Calthurst holds, and which he so cleverly got possession of, is only a copy, not the original," and turning on his heel, with a contemptuous sneer upon his lip, he left the office.

For several minutes after the departure of Sir Herbert Delme not a word was spoken by father or son. Sad and sorrowful they both sat, communing with their own thoughts, till the latter, in a voice tremulous with emotion, and stretching out his hand and grasping that of his father, which lay upon the table, said, " Father, dear father, can you forgive your erring son ? "

" Yes, my child," said his father, tears stealing down his cheeks, and gazing fondly into his son's pale, haggard features. " Yes ; or I should not be a believer in what our divine Saviour has taught us ; " and drawing his son towards him, he embraced him with deep feeling and emotion.

John Calthurst's heart was full to overflowing, he pressed his father's hand to his heart. In his secret soul he loathed the past, and vowed that the future should atone for the past, sincerely thanking that God who had rescued him from a miserable doom. It was some time before father and son recovered sufficient composure to converse calmly, but at length John Calthurst gave his father a clear statement of all that had appeared mysterious in recent events.

It will be quite unnecessary to state to

our readers how from the infatuation of play
John Calthurst became the victim of the crafty
and unscrupulous Sir Herbert Delme — for
John Calthurst had an excellent heart, was
very talented, and dearly loved his father and
all his family. Sir Herbert plunged him in
debt, chiefly to himself, by pretended loans of
John Calthurst's own money, which he had
won unfairly, assisted by confederates.

We must entirely exonerate him from the
scheme of stealing the will; that was Adams's
own project. After it was stolen—and it was
only when John Calthurst was overwhelmed
with debt and led to drink, that he became
aware of it—Sir Herbert's sophistry overcame
all his scruples, he pointed out to him the
grandeur of his succeeding to the Mortimer
estates, and his marriage with his sister.

To have a brother-in-law a baronet, and
the possessor of such riches, blinded him to
every result that might occur from his connection with the schemes of Sir Herbert
Delme and the clerk Adams. After the ab-

straction of the will, Adams and Sir Herbert had a very serious quarrel. Adams considered himself wronged and ill requited. The night before his flight from London, he had a private interview with John Calthurst.

" I shall never return to this country," said Adams; " I have wronged your father, who was my benefactor: take this packet," handing him a sealed paper of some bulk, " keep it, and promise not to open it till you find yourself treated by Sir Herbert as he has perfidiously treated me,—and now farewell."

The young man contrived to evade all pursuit, and finally succeeded in getting to America. John Calthurst was not yet enlightened as to the baronet's true character; if he were he was blinded by his marriage with his sister and the certainty, as it then appeared, of his succeeding to the Mortimer estates. At length John's debts and entanglements increased so greatly, and his applications to Sir Herbert for funds to liquidate his liabilities were so pressing, that one night, when half mad from losses in play, he accepted a bill for five thousand pounds, drawn up by Sir Herbert Delme, which he declared he would get cashed, and before it would become due he should be able to take it up.

The next night John Calthurst tempted fortune with the baronet in a low disreputable gambling house, and lost a considerable sum. Sir Herbert insidiously induced him to drink, and when in a state of mind as to care little what he did, Sir Herbert induced him to sign his father's name to a bill for five thousand pounds, at three months, which he said would set all right.

The next day the young man awoke to a sense of his horrible situation. At length a little retrospect of his past conduct awoke in him a feeling of intense disgust and bitter remorse; his first thought was to rush to Sir Herbert, and demand the bill back. He met the baronet coming to him.

"You must go to Jacob Jacobs, this moment," said Sir Herbert, "he has got the bill you signed with your father's name, and from some unaccountable reason refuses to cash it at forty per cent., without seeing you. Go quickly, if you wish to save yourself from exposure," and without giving the horrified young man time to reply, Sir Herbert Delme drove off. For a moment, John Calthurst stood appalled—his first thought was to put an end to himself; but he was, as he thanked God the moment after, not so lost as to commit that last condemning act of a madman. He then hurried off to Jacob Jacobs, the broker, a man notorious for extortion and usury; yet many a worse man existed than Jacob Jacobs.

John Calthurst tried to appear calm and unconcerned, as he entered Jacob Jacobs' office. He was alone, and looking up from his desk, he let his keen, piercing, clear, grey eye rest upon the solicitor's son.

" Mr. Jacobs," said John Calthurst, quietly, " Sir Herbert Delme has left in your hands a bill, accepted by my father, and payable at

Burden, Fife, and Co., bankers, at three months."

"Did the baronet say it was a three month's bill," said the broker.

"Yes; at least, I understood it was for three months," returned John Calthurst.

Jacob Jacobs unlocked his desk, and took out a folded paper. Unrolling it, he said, "This is a cheque, not a bill, signed by your father, for five thousand pounds, payable to bearer at sight."

John Calthurst felt sick, and turned, if possible, more deadly pale than he was already.

"Now I tell you what, Mr. Calthurst," said the broker, "this is a forgery; it was never signed by your respectable father: it's a forgery! When I present this at the bank upon which it is drawn it will be stopped as a forgery, for though the signature is tolerably well, it will be detected. Nevertheless, I was taken in by your clever friend, Sir Herbert Delme; he got a thousand pounds out of me on this cheque, on account, giving a very plausible reason why he did not present it himself. Now, I tell you what, Mr. John Calthurst, you signed this cheque. If I present it, you are ruined. But I tell you what I will do—bring me a thousand pounds before four o'clock, and I will give you back this cheque, and bless your stars at your escape, and take a usurer's—I know I am called a usurer, and I am to spendthrifts and unprincipled scoundrels—but take my advice, and though Sir Herbert Delme is your brother-in-law, cease all intercourse with him for the future."

John Calthurst hurried out of the broker's office, made the best of his way to his father's office, with the intention of throwing himself at his feet, and confessing all ; but as he stood by the door, trembling and hesitating, Lieut. Chamberlain came along the passage. A sudden thought struck him. Our readers know the result of his interview with our hero. Furnished with a cheque for a thousand pounds, he hurried to the bank, cashed it, and then hastened to the brokers.

Jacob Jacobs took the money and gave up the cheque, John Calthurst trembling with agitation and emotion.

"Did you tell your father?" asked the broker.

"No," said the young man, " I wish to spare him that blow."

" Ah !" said Jacob Jacobs, " too late ; the baronet was here, and thought it was all right, and wanted a couple of thousands more. He got into a furious passion, and swore he would go that instant to your father, and if he did not fork out five thousand pounds, on your own note, which he held, he would expose the forgery you committed—excuse my plain speaking. What has passed shall never be spoken of by me. Go to your father, he is a just and honourable man; he will forgive you. Break off all connection with your unworthy friend, Sir Herbert."

Smarting with this fresh baseness of his

brother-in-law, John Calthurst hurried to the office, opened a private desk of his own, and broke open the packet given him by Adams. On a slip of paper was written, " The inside is the original will of Mr. Mortimer ; the one destroyed before Sir Herbert's face was an exact copy." Rushing into his father's office, the scene took place recorded in the preceding pages.

The foregoing is a brief outline of the rather long explanatory narrative of John Calthurst, when he brought from his private desk the packet given him by Adams.

" You will see at once, my dear father, that this is the original will. Adams had it carefully copied, no doubt, for some ulterior object. He had a singular talent for imitating signatures, after a few minutes' study of the writing. As Sir Herbert Delme could have no knowledge of the signatures to the will, he felt satisfied when he saw it burned before his face that it was all right. I see by this will that you become entitled to ten thousand pounds, whether Miss Mortimer succeeds to the property or not. Thank God Adams had the gratitude to restore it. It will more than pay for the losses incurred by my sad delusion, and Adams's baseness. I will work, dear father, and repay this sum, as your clerk; and will only take a clerk's salary till my future conduct prove I am deserving of your confidence and affection."

Seeing his father much affected, and inclined to dispute this resolution, he said, "On this point, dear father, I am resolved. I have too much to be thankful and grateful to Providence for to feel this a hardship."

The kind-hearted solicitor felt so relieved, that he embraced his son with tenderness, told him he would forget all, and let him follow the bent of his inclinations. "We must replace the one thousand pounds that noble, generous hearted sailor so freely lent you. I will write out a cheque; at once repay the money, and seek an opportunity to thank him for his disinterested kindness."

John Calthurst then gave his father the will of Mr. Mortimer, who saw at a glance that it was the original document.

"I cannot," said Mr. Calthurst, "comprehend Adams's conduct. Taking the will must have been the impulse of the moment, when the opportunity offered by my losing my keys."

"I tell you how it was, sir. Adams became unprincipled from losses at play and association with Sir Herbert Delme. You happened to call him into your office one day when you had Mr. Mortimer's will upon the table. He perceived, and noticed it; but would never have thought more of it, if the news of the loss of the Mortimer family had not excited Sir Herbert Delme into the sanguine hope of succeeding to Mr. Mortimer's wealth. Meeting the baronet at one of the low gambling houses, Sir Herbert spoke exultingly of his prospects. 'But,' said Adams, 'are you aware that there is a will in the possession of Mr. Calthurst?'

" Sir Herbert was confounded ; for he well
knew that if his uncle had kept a will, it had
been made to cut him off from inheriting his
fortune. He at once offered Adams five thousand pounds for the will.   But Adams told him
it was impossible to get it from the iron chest
in which it was kept. As you already know,
a chance accident threw your keys into his
hands. He had plenty of time, and he ex-
tracted the will.

" Sir Herbert had not sufficient funds to
pay him ; and, after some delay, and much
bickering between them, the baronet paid one
thousand ; and Adams burned, in his presence,
a copy, instead of the original, forged your
name to several documents, raised money on
them, fled to Liverpool, and embarked
for America. I feel miserable and humiliated
when I recall these disgraceful events.
Blinded by a false ambition, and spurred on
into crime by fresh entanglements, I should
have fallen a victim to my insane infatuation,
had not Sir Herbert himself inspired me

with a feeling of disgust against the career I was pursuing; and a night of anguish and remorse restored me to a keen sense of my desperate situation, and caused a determination in my own mind to cast off for ever the baneful hold ambition and love of play had upon me."

CHAPTER XI.

LIEUTENANT CHAMBERLAIN and Mr. Hawkins met at Mrs. Penson's, two or three days after the events recorded in our last chapter. They greeted each other with cordiality, for Mr. Hawkins felt a most earnest attachment for the young lieutenant, who told Mr. Hawkins that he had solicited a berth for him on board the Leander, he himself being made second lieutenant; but when he informed his friend that Lord Linwood was his uncle, he exclaimed,

"Ah, I see it all now. He could not well make a commander of you, without your serving some little time as a first lieutenant.

You may depend on it you will have a step the first engagement you take a part in."

"Always provided, my friend," returned our hero, "that we do not lose the number of our mess."

"Well, yes," said Mr. Hawkins, "granted ; I am proud to enter the service again, and also at the prospect of serving under such a commander as the captain of the Leander."

The conversation then turned upon their prizes, the Belle Poule, the cutter, and the corvette. "I have heard," said Mr. Hawkins, "while waiting in Plymouth, that all naval men considered the corvette a re- markably beautiful craft, but undermasted, and too lightly armed. I suppose they will put twelve-pounders, instead of eight, into her, and a couple of long twenty-four-pound carronades. These additions would make her nearly equal to a frigate."

Having conversed for a considerable time upon their own affairs, our hero and his com- panion joined Mrs. Penson and Rose in the parlour, where tea and coffee were ready on the table.

Our hero took an opportunity to ask Mrs. Penson if she had ever heard where his father and mother were married.

" Indeed, my dear, I cannot tell you that," said Mrs. Penson, " for I never heard either your mother or father speak on the subject; but I am quite satisfied that Captain Thompson will be able to tell you if he is alive."

" Oh, yes; he is alive. He commands the Leander, so I shall have every opportunity of questioning him when I join."

" I hope you will hear from France before you sail," observed Rose. " It must have been a great trial to Miss Mortimer, your leaving. She is now entirely amongst strangers and foreigners."

" Fortunately," said Lieutenant Chamberlain, " she has a staunch friend in Mademoiselle de Morni. In ten days, at furthest, we expect to have intelligence."

It was late when our hero and Mr. Hawkins

left the cottage to return to London. Mr. Hawkins was to remain till our hero received his instructions, and then they would both leave together for Plymouth. A day or two after his visit to Mrs. Penson, our hero received a note from Lord Linwood, requesting him to call at Grosvenor House the following day, at twelve o'clock precisely. He was punctual. The admiral received him exceedingly kind, though he appeared very serious. Requesting our hero to be seated his lordship said, "Perhaps, Mr. Chamberlain, you are not very well acquainted with the early history of your father and mother?"

"No, my lord," returned our hero, "not very well; in fact, I have had little opportunity of inquiring into their past history."

"Are you aware that your mother was an Elphinstone?" asked his lordship, "and consequently connected with the Linwood family —in fact, that your mother was my sister?"

"I was not aware such was the case, my lord, till I returned to England a few days ago."

"And pray may I ask who made you acquainted with this fact?"

"A Mrs. Penson, my lord, to whose care I was consigned by Captain Thompson, who was left my guardian. She was greatly attached to my poor mother, who, deserted and disowned by her relatives, found attention and affection from—"

"I beg," interrupted Lord Linwood, his dark brows contracting, "that you will keep your opinion of your mother's conduct to yourself. When a high and noble name is disgraced by a marriage —"

"My lord, pardon me," firmly, but respectfully, interrupted our hero, "I am your nephew, but permit me to say that the name of Chamberlain, though not dignified by titles, is a good and honourable name, and has never been disgraced by my lamented father, who died serving his country, and left a gallant name and deeds to his son to imitate."

"I am afraid, young gentleman,'' said Lord Linwood, rather severely, " that you have imbibed, in your short career, some of the levelling revolutionary ideas of the French people. You appear to look upon rank and station as mere words of sound."

" No, my lord; but I revere my father's name, and would not exchange it for the highest in the land."

" You are young," said the admiral, after a moment's pause, and in a kinder tone. " I do not want to quarrel with a son because he defends his father. There," and he held out his hand, "I acknowledge you as my nephew, and no doubt you will be my successor to the honours and titles of the Linwoods, for, I am sorry to say, I heard this morning that my brother the earl is in bad health, and not likely to survive a severe fit."

Astonished, our hero took Admiral Linwood's hand. His lordship drew him gently towards him, embraced him affectionately, and with some emotion, as he said, " I have had my eyes upon you ever since you entered the navy, and heard of all your actions; and I am very happy to say your good conduct and gallantry have rendered you worthy of the rank you are, if spared, likely to attain. I am going to-morrow to Linwood Castle, to see my brother. Come to dinner to-day; I wish to introduce you to your aunt and cousin, and as you cannot have any pressing engagement, I should wish you to accompany me to Linwood. The earl will, if not too ill, be glad to see his only nephew."

The young man was completely confounded by this most unexpected change in his fortunes and destiny. Nevertheless, he greatly pleased his uncle by the manner and the language he made use of to express his feelings at this unhoped for restoration to the affection and esteem of his mother's family. Taking an affectionate leave of his uncle, promising to be punctual to the hour of seven, he descended the stairs. As he was leaving the house, Phœbe Marks tripped across the hall and handed him a small note, and then, with a very knowing look, returned the way she came.

On gaining some distance from the house, our hero opened the note; it contained only a few lines, as follows—"I am so rejoiced, dear cousin, at your reception by your uncle; he spoke last night to my aunt of his intention of acknowledging you. Not one sign of having seen me before. Meet me as a total stranger.—Your cousin Flora." Our hero began to think that his poor cousin Flora must have a difficult game to play. He could very well imagine that she was attached to some one not at all in accordance with the views of her guardians. "It seems," thought our hero, "that the daughters of the house of Linwood are never to have a will of their own, in love affairs, at all events."

So extremely absorbed was the sailor by his thoughts, and scarcely heeding the number of persons he passed, that he came with some force against a gentleman who was leaving a shop to enter a carriage standing beside the flags. Raising his hat, he was about to make an apology for his inattention, when the person against whom he had run, said in a savage tone—

" You have done this purposely to insult me, sir."

Our hero looked into the face of Sir Herbert Delme, whom he at once recognised, saying, very quietly, " You can scarcely, Sir Herbert, imagine that ; I can have no possible motive for insulting you, and was going to apologise for my inattention."

" Curse your inattention and apology too," returned the baronet; " I want no apology from you—I take this as an insult, and shall expect satisfaction for it. I know your name, but not your residence."

" Upon my word, Sir Herbert," returned our hero with a smile, seeing they were getting rapidly surrounded by a crowd, " You must be singularly fond of quarrelling, when you seek for an excuse to fight with a man who is willing to make you an apology for a trifling inattention. But I will not baulk you—there is my card, and at the same time let me tell you your conduct is quite unbecoming a gentleman, and that what I now say cannot and will not be retracted ;" so saying, he pushed aside the few persons pressing close upon them, and who, having heard all that passed, gave him a cheer as he quietly pursued his way to his hotel. In his sitting-room he found Mr. Hawkins waiting for him.

"Well, my good friend," said our hero, "I am just at this moment particularly glad to see you."

" Why, what has happened, my dear sir?" asked Mr. Hawkins, anxiously.

Lieutenant Chamberlain then told his friend the particulars of his interview with Lord Linwood, which delighted the honest sailor, who is most truly attached to our hero. " But there's something else to come," he anxiously enquired.

" Oh, yes, my friend, there is ; but it does not give me the slightest trouble or care,

except on account of my going into the
country to-morrow—but you will do what's
wanting in my absence." He then told him
his rencontre with Sir Herbert Delme just as
it occurred.

"Well, by Jove, if that's not the coolest
piece of impertinence and vindictiveness I
have ever heard of" said Mr. Hawkins. "I
remember you told me you picked this confounded baronet the other day from between
two kicking horses, at the risk of getting
kicked by them yourself, and the ungrateful
cur fastened a quarrel upon you for nothing.
What can he hope to gain by a duel with
you?"

"Faith, it would puzzle anyone to tell," said
our hero; "unless to gratify his malice against
me, for being a witness in court the other day.
I know no other cause. It's not worth
troubling our heads about, beyond this,
you must take up your quarters here till I
return to Linwood Castle; the baronet will
send some one here to-morrow, no doubt;

you can fix time and place; I don't care where
it is, or how it's to be. If he does not kill or
disable me before I fire, depend upon it I will
leave him a remembrance of me that he will
not easily forget, for he has insisted upon this
duel purposely."

John Hawkins by no means relished this
affair, not because he feared for our hero's
life; he knew he was a remarkably good shot,
and as cool under any circumstances of peril
as any man living. But he did not consider
himself a sufficiently responsible person, not
the equal in rank of his principal; and he
eared not acting as became his principal's station in society, especially now that Lieut.
Chamberlain was the acknowledged nephew
of Lord Linwood, and next in succession to
the title.

" What the deuce are you thinking of,
Hawkins," said our hero, as he finished
writing a note to Rose Talbot, stating that he
was going into the country for a day or two
to see his uncle, the Earl of Linwood.

" Well, I was thinking, sir," said the mate,
" that I wish I had to thrash that baronet
after my own fashion, instead of your putting
yourself in the way of a stray bullet, to gratify
the pique of such a consequential puppy.   I
should like you to go and meet this baronet
with a better man than myself—I mean in
rank and station, sir.   The baronet's friend
may object to me as a non-commissioned
officer."

" Stuff and nonsense, Hawkins; a man
that has stood a shower of grape and canister
in a dozen engagements to be objected to by
an empty-headed civilian, is too much of a
joke.   Treat whatever anyone says on that
subject with contempt; tell whoever comes
that you are my friend, and if he likes, we will
give them two shots each for our one, and
if that doesn't please him, tell him to take
himself off.   I shall know how to manage him when I come back. There are one or
two of the officers of the Pelican in town, but
I have not time to hunt them up now."

"Ah," said Mr. Hawkins, " I can find Lieut. Spencer, of the Pelican, if I want him. I met him yesterday, and he was very glad to see me—had heard of our capture of the corvette, and wished us better luck still : he's the man to go out with you, a better fellow never lived."

"By Jove, you are right there, Hawkins, so just please yourself if you find yourself in any difficulty, as neither you nor I ever had anything of the kind on our hands before. I hate the thing myself: duelling is a hateful custom. If a man offends, if he's a gentleman, he will feel no scruples in apologising. Your regular duellist is a pest to society, and I strongly suspect that Sir Herbert Delme walks in the steps of his father, who was notorious for his duels, and his crack shooting; and yet he was killed by a man who never fired a shot in anger in his whole life."

At the appointed time our hero proceeded to Lord Linwood's mansion in a hackney coach. When shown up into the drawing-room, and announced, he was received by the admiral's sister, Lady Edgehill, in a very courtly and dignified style. Nevertheless, she welcomed him as her nephew, and embraced him, touching his cheek with her lips, and then sitting down, pointed to a seat beside her.

"I am very happy to find, nephew," said her ladyship, "that your career in the navy is highly approved of by your uncle, the admiral, and I congratulate you on your future prospects."

"I am rejoiced, aunt," returned our hero, gaily, and quite undisturbed by the formal tone and manner of the stately dame, who kept her cold grey eyes fixed upon him, "that my good fortune has secured me such patronage, and hope to continue to deserve the admiral's esteem."

As he ceased speaking, the door opened, and two young ladies entered, both elegantly and tastefully attired; but quite dissimilar in their style of beauty, though both were lovely. Lady Edgehill rose, and introduced the two fair girls as her nieces. The tallest, as the niece of her late husband, was introduced as the Lady Georgina Deveaux. The young girl bent gracefully, but at the same time cast a very inquisitive glance upon Lieut. Chamberlain. There was a world of meaning in that glance, and then she sat down.

" This young lady," continued her ladyship, introducing Flora, " is your cousin, Flora Smith;" she laid a strong emphasis on the latter word. " You have met before, I dare say you remember, nephew; but I suppose at that time you were not aware you were speaking to so near a relative, though what Miss Flora wanted with you, puzzles me at this time."

" Indeed, aunt," interrupted Flora, with a merry laugh, " there was no great mystery intended. I was aware Lieut. Chamberlain was my cousin, and I naturally longed to tell him so, though I knew it was not strictly etiquette for me to be the first to announce it."

" The knowledge that I have so charming a cousin," said our hero, taking Flora's hand, and gallantly kissing it, "is the most agreeable tidings I have known for years," he then led his cousin to a seat near Lady Georgina, and sat down beside the two fair girls, and the conversation became more general. Lady Georgina appeared to possess a high spirit, and great animation.

" I am sorry to say, nephew, that you will not see your uncle to-night. The Earl of Linwood is so much better, that he has given up his journey to-morrow to Linwood Castle. The admiral meets some of the cabinet ministers to-night, and has gone to an early and select dinner party at Lord D——'s. The house will sit late to-night."

Dinner being announced broke up the conversation. During the meal, which was in every way *récherché*, the conversation turned upon various subjects, of little real importance, but showed that Lady Edgehill could unbend and be extremely agreeable ; and also that the two fair girls were exceedingly dangerous companions for any young lieutenant, who had a heart to bestow.

In the evening the piano and harp were put in requisition, the instruments being played with taste and skill by both young ladies. As our hero, who was passionately fond of music, and was turning over the pages of a popular song for the Lady Georgina, she suddenly paused, turned on her stool, and said, with great animation, "Only think, we are alone, your aunt has left the room, Flora."

"So she has, I declare," responded Flora.

"Now, Mr. Chamberlain," said Lady Georgina, looking our surprised hero in the face, with an arch smile ; " do not think me a madcap. If you do I cannot help it. But tell me, what do you think I was brought here for this evening? You are puzzled, Mr. Chamberlain, and well you may. I will tell you,

I was invited here that you might fall in love with me. What do you think of that?"

"Why," returned our hero, with a smile, and rather an increase of colour; "that such an event was very likely to occur, if—"

"Ah, there it is—if—" interrupted the merry girl. "If you were not already engaged to a young, and I understand, a most lovely girl, now a prisoner in France."

Her companion looked amazed.

"You see I know all about you; we are connections if we are not relatives, and did I not know as much as I do in reality, I should never think of acting as I am now doing; but listen to me seriously, for much depends on our actions whether our future prospects will be all sunshine, or darkened by clouds."

"Depend on it," said our hero, warmly, "that anything I can do by word or act shall have your future happiness and that of my cousin Flora in prospective."

"I am sure of that," replied Flora, affectionately; "the fact is we have both disposed of our hearts without consulting our guardians."

"Do, dear Flora," said Lady Georgina, "sit down to the piano; you can play and listen while I explain our plans to your cousin."

Flora commenced a quiet melody, whilst Lady Georgina addressed our hero.

"Your uncle and aunt have planned a match between us, which they consider every way eligible ; and so it might, if the fates had not decreed otherwise. According to the inevitable decrees of destiny, the Linwoods are doomed to experience defeat in all their matrimonial speculations. With an intense horror of the daughters of Linwood, or any female connection marrying out of their own station, they adopt probably the very means that—intending to secure them— baffle their intentions. Lord Linwood is my guardian. In twelve or fourteen months I shall be my own mistress ; till then I wish to keep my wishes and intentions quiet. They

have set their hearts upon a union between
us, and they have also actually affianced
your cousin Flora to a gentleman every way
unexceptional; but, alas! not to her mind,
she having already disposed of her affections.
Now let me tell you that to all intents and
purposes you must let your worthy aunt and
uncle suppose that you are very much in
love with me. That's what you must do.
Leave the rest of the performance for me,
and depend on it you shall get out of the
scrape without blame. If you attempt to
tell your uncle and aunt that you are engaged
to a young lady, and that young lady not a
patrician, adieu to your commandership for
years. Such a confession, besides would cause
a breach between you and your powerful
relative, who has the power to disinherit
you—"

"But, pardon me, my dear Lady Georgina," interrupted our surprised hero. "Why
should the anger of your guardians fall upon
you; it would be a weakness in me to save

myself by false appearances, and leave you to bear the responsibility."

"In love and war, my gallant friend," said the young lady, with a merry laugh, "strategem and artifice are allowable. I shall be of age, as I before told you, in one more year; I shall then be entitled to a very considerable inheritance. I am engaged to an honourable gentleman, of very good family, and an officer in the army. Your pretty cousin, Flora, has embarked her heart in the same venture, but unfortunately she is not an heiress, and she is my junior by nearly two years. If we had time we undoubtedly should have made you our father confessor, but we have not; therefore, when my guardian, Lord Linwood, asks you what you think of Georgina Deveaux, you had better say all you would say had the fates designed us for each other. Leave it to me to decline the honour of your alliance, and all will go well."

"Hush!" exclaimed Flora. "I hear my aunt's step. I will play louder."

The next moment Lady Edgehill entered the room; in a little time they sat down to supper, after which our hero took leave of his aunt and the two girls, very much bewildered and puzzled by the events of the evening.

END OF VOL. II.

T. C. Newby, 30, Welbeck Street, Cavendish Square, London.

WILSON'S
PATENT DRAWING-ROOM
BAGATELLE AND BILLIARD TABLES,
WITH REVERSIBLE TOPS.
Circular, Oblong, Oval, and other Shapes, in various Sizes,
FORMING A HANDSOME TABLE.

Patent Bagatelle Table—Open.	Patent Bagatelle Table—Closed.
Prices from 5 to 25 Guineas.	**Prospectus Free by post.**

WILSON AND CO., PATENTEES,
Cabinet Makers, Upholsterers, House Agents, Undertakers, &c.,

18, WIGMORE STREET (Corner of Welbeck Street), LONDON, W.; also at the

MANUFACTURING COURT, CRYSTAL PALACE, SYDENHAM.

In 1 Vol. Price 12s.

ON CHANGE OF CLIMATE,
A GUIDE FOR TRAVELLERS IN PURSUIT OF HEALTH.
BY THOMAS MORE MADDEN, M.D., M.R.C.S. ENG.

Illustrative of the Advantages of the various localities resorted to by
Invalids, for the cure or alleviation of chronic diseases, especially
consumption. With Observations on Climate, and its Influences
on Health and Disease, the result of extensive personal experience
of many Southern Climes.

SPAIN, PORTUGAL, ALGERIA, MOROCCO, FRANCE, ITALY,
THE MEDITERRANEAN ISLANDS, EGYPT, &c.

" Dr. Madden has been to most of the places he describes, and his
book contains the advantage of a guide, with the personal experience
of a traveller. To persons who have determined that they ought to
have change of climate, we can recommend Dr. Madden as a guide."
—*Athenæum.*

" It contains much valuable information respecting various
favorite places of resort, and is evidently the work of a well-informed
physician."—*Lancet.*

" Dr. Madden's book deserves confidence—a most accurate and
excellent work."—*Dublin Medical Review.*

THE

GENERAL FURNISHING

AND

UPHOLSTERY COMPANY

(LIMITED),

F. J. ACRES, MANAGER,

24 and 25, Baker Street, W.

———

The Company are now Exhibiting all the most approved Novelties
of the Season in

CARPETS, CHINTZES,

MUSLIN CURTAINS,

And every variety of textile fabric for Upholstery purposes
constituting the most recherché selection in the trade.

TEETH WITHOUT PAIN AND WITHOUT SPRINGS.
OSTEO EIDON FOR ARTIFICIAL TEETH,
EQUAL TO NATURE.

Complete Sets £4 4s., £7 7s., £10 10s., £15 15s., and £21.

SINGLE TEETH AND PARTIAL SETS AT PROPORTIONATELY
MODERATE CHARGES.

A: PERFECT FIT GUARANTEED.

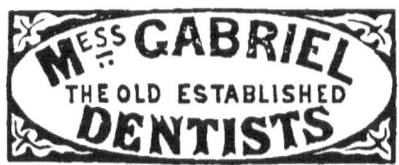

London:
27, HARLEY STREET, CAVENDISH SQUARE, W.
134, DUKE STREET, LIVERPOOL.
65, NEW STREET, BIRMINGHAM.

CITY ADDRESS :
64, LUDGATE HILL, 64.
(4 doors from the Railway Bridge).

ONLY ONE VISIT REQUIRED FROM COUNTRY PATIENTS.

Gabriel's Treatise on the Teeth, explaining their patented mode
of supplying Teeth without Springs or Wires, may be had gratis
on application, or free by post.

THE TOILET.—A due attention to the gifts and graces of the person, and a becoming preservation of the advantages of nature, are of more value and importance with reference to our health and well-being, than many parties are inclined to suppose. Several of the most attractive portions of the human frame are delicate and fragile, in proportion as they are graceful and pleasing; and the due conservation of them is intimately associated with our health and comfort. The hair, for example, from the delicacy of its growth and texture, and its evident sympathy with the emotions of the mind; the skin, with its intimate relation to the most vital of our organs, as those of respiration, circulation and digestion, together with the delicacy and susceptibility of its own texture; and the teeth, also, from their peculiar structure, formed as they are, of bone or dentine, and cased with a fibrous investment of enamel; these admirable and highly essential portions of our frames, are all to be regarded not merely as objects of external beauty and display, but as having an intimate relation to our health, and the due discharge of the vital functions. The care of them ought never to be entrusted to ignorant or unskilful hands; and it is highly satisfactory to point out as protectors of these vital portions of our frame the preparations which have emanated from the laboratories of the Messrs. Rowlands, their unrivalled Macassar for the hair, their Kalydor for improving and beautifying the complexion, and their Odonto for the teeth and gums.

NEW NOVELS IN THE PRESS.

In Three Vols.

IT MAY BE TRUE.

By MRS. WOOD.

In Three Vols.

TREASON AT HOME.

By MRS. GREENOUGH.

BEDSTEADS, BEDDING, AND BED ROOM FURNITURE.

HEAL & SON'S

Show Rooms contain a large assortment of Brass Bedsteads, suitable both for home use and for Tropical Climates.

Handsome Iron Bedsteads, with Brass Mountings, and elegantly Japanned.

Plain Iron Bedsteads for Servants.

Every description of Woodstead, in Mahogany, Birch, and Walnut Tree Woods, Polished Deal and Japanned, all fitted with Bedding and Furnitures complete.

Also, every description of Bed Room Furniture, consisting of Wardrobes, Chests of Drawers, Washstands, Tables, Chairs, Sofas, Couches, and every article for the complete furnishing of a Bed Room.

AN

ILLUSTRATED CATALOGUE,

Containing Designs and Prices of 150 articles of Bed Room Furniture, as well as of 100 Bedsteads, and Prices of every description of Bedding

Sent Free by Post.

HEAL & SON,

BEDSTEAD, BEDDING,

AND

BED ROOM FURNITURE MANUFACTURERS

196, TOTTENHAM COURT ROAD,

LONDON. W.